Whispers of Winter

II

An Anthology

Edited by T.L. Williams

Whispers of Winter II: An Anthology

Published by Zorb Press

Version 1.0

Cover design by Ayd Instone.

ISBN: 9798770332414

www.justtlwilliams.wordpress.com

In memory of all those who lost their lives to the Coronavirus disease.

CONTENTS

5

Winter Poems

Winter Stories

Recipes

Occasional Pieces

FOREWORD BY T.L. WILLIAMS

It has been said that, 'Often good can come out of bad'. In the case of the anthology, the first volume was born as a result of the Coronavirus halting my plans to put on a local community pantomime to raise money for two local charities, Donnington Doorstep Family Centre, and The Porch day centre. I am pleased to say that the first volume of 'Whispers of Winter' and later, my original pantomime, 'Spectre Avenue' (performed in October 2021 with my heartfelt thanks to my co-director, our superb cast, crew, creative team, tech team, *Glitter Patrol & Co* band, *Strawberry Faye Majorettes* dance troupe, Cowley Workers' social club, and stupendous audience), were both wonderful successes raising superb funds for the aforementioned charities.

Due to the touching encouragement and feedback I received from readers and contributors of the first anthology, I decided to endeavour to put together volume ii.

It has been a joyful experience liaising with writers to compile this second volume. I have had the pleasure and privilege of conversing with contributors over email, a brief skype meeting, and in person, including a delightful school visit. I would like to thank each and every one of these people for the time and work they spent to give to this book.

The enthusiasm and passion of the writers who have contributed to this volume has been a joy, as has reading their pieces which spread across the vast spectrum of 'Winter' as a genre.

On a more serious note, I think it is important to remember those who were sadly affected by the awful virus; the victims it claimed and their families and friends. That is why this year, all profit raised from the sales of this volume will benefit Cruse Bereavement Support, who help people affected by grief, by offering advice, information, and support.

(You can learn more about the charity here: www.cruse.org.uk).

Thank you to you the reader for choosing to purchase this anthology, I hope you enjoy reading it as much as I have done putting it together.

In keeping with last year, let's toast, to '*winter*' this time, and to all the magic, wonderment, and warmth we find within it.

- T. L. Williams.

Winter Pieces from the Students of Cherwell School Writing Club

Winter's Heart

A screeching owl call, filling the sky,
No trace of leaves, golden and dry.
A whispered secret of magic and more,
From the tops of the trees to the frostbitten floor.

The colours in the sky, all golden and bright,
Spill into darkness, into inky black night.
The moon comes out and peers down below,
Onto trees, buildings, and ground dusted with snow.

The stars disappear in the new coming light,
And birds start to sing and sweep into flight.
Both darkness and light the world wears like a crown,
And with the flurry of birds the owl dives down.

Evie Galligan

' . '

A frozen crystal pulsates in this dry cage of ice

Slaving away by command of the blizzard above

Its shards piercing into the bars that hold it still

Slaving away by command of the   drifting white
thing they call hope

Sputtering and lurching till the cage breaks away

Coughing and stalling till the smoke takes the shape

Of my fears

Winter has come

Claire Sussussi Yindom

14

A Winter Poem

Through a weeping window I watched thousands
of grey needles relentlessly batter pools of saturated
grass;
I watched as the wet wintry wind swept torrents
in a harsh crescendo of staccato drops against the wall.

Through the icy glass, the smell of cold still hung to
me.
Biting. Bitter. Bleak.
The dark clouds were obscured by the lashing rain;
the sky a mirror of the black miry ground.

Now the long fingers of dawn illuminate the freely
falling snow,
and shine upon the cold crisp carpet and frost
that delicately envelops every leaf of an evergreen,
atop which a round robin springs into the air.

Now the pale blue sky reflects in the shimmering
streams,
and heat from the impromptu sun of a fire warms the
air
and thins the snow, revealing a yellow winter clematis:
a relic from some other time.

Soon we'll be able to stroll in puffy overcoats,
immune to the insignificant nip of the breeze, as we'll
walk

to pull from the snow a sodden orange leaf;
to climb a slope to fall or tumble back down.

Soon we'll watch the birds flurry in front of a glowing
sunset,
watch more flowers emerge from the white sea,
watch silhouettes of leaves float and flutter in the air,
and we'll sit placidly in the white land of Winter.

Ben Ross

When the World Froze Around Me

Scorching yet blistering.
I traverse around the smoky wasteland,
Composed of soft
Yet towering dark bark.
As their razor claws
Entangled between each other.
I was overshadowed
By their wispy smile.

Crunch and chomp.
The gravel-like snow played
A crackly yet
Soothing beat.
My dreary leather boots,
Sinking
Into the deep crevice of the
Vast jaws.

I stumbled upon
The grandeur cemetery.
Thick shadows
Suffocating light
As the stone walls glared over my sight.
I began to enter the smiling gate
Suddenly gazing upon
The rows and rows of graves.

One grave ingrained in my mind
Like a slimy leech,
Radiating warmth
From my paralysed blood.
The words,
Written on all of the rows of graves,
More bitter than the rising blistering
From the jaws of the dark clouds.

"Even when the world freezes around you,
My mind will radiate with the warmth of your
heart."

The growing walls
Overshadowed the light as
The beating heart
Echoed around the darkening mists
As I sprinted and galloped
Like a great stallion
About to be clawed
By the jaws of the dark clouds...

Cian Huckins

'The World Can Change Its Heart'

Winter majestic and humbling,
wrapped in its cloak of crisp cool air.
Winter a keeper of beauty, just like the other seasons.
Although, none like winter.

We are all connected,
Connected to winter,
Connected through the beauty we *all* hold.

'No scars; We're beautiful,
We're stars, and we're beautiful' - just the way we are.

Through cuts and bruises we shine.
Decorated in black, purples and blue over tear-
streaked faces.
Through marks and burns we shine.
Covered in pain over disappointed and despairing
eyes.
Coated in misery we stand, we shine.

Brought together by song and joy
Together in silent support
United.

The frosty chill air of winter,
Thick and dense with mystery within its fog.
Shrouded to the eye's wonder, astonishment, surprise.
Behind countless barriers.

'No scars; We're beautiful
We're stars, and we're beautiful' - just the way we are.

Our 'scars' are our medals,
medals to be worn with pride.
Our imperfections are our unique qualities,
without them we are no different.
Difference makes us whole,
for who are we but different?
While different, united
While united, unique.

'We don't have to change a thing
The world can change its heart'
Just as the chilling snow coated mountains glistening
in early morning sun are different,
Different to the overpowering colour-filled landscape
filled with the essence of spring
Different to the blazing heat of a mid-day's sun and
humid air filled with the luxuries of summer
Different to the fiery flame-coloured trees and strong
gusts of wind carrying the entity of autumn.

Different; unique; united.

Sharin Poongaran

20

The Winter King by Ted Boulter

In the isolated hills of Northern Russia, where the days are cold and short, there lies a small village, and looming over it, Bram Castle. Long ago in days of old, a tyrant King ruled over this castle and the village. He was a cruel, horrible leader, taking no care for his people, only what was on his plate that night. Finally, with age overcoming him, he was ready for death to make his bedside visit. Not long before he eased into eternal sleep, however, he forced his witches to cast a spell over him that would wake him from this end. The witches warned him of the consequences of his actions, but he took no notice. With the spell cast, he finally slipped into the sleep of death. The people celebrated.

"Finally! It's over!" they cried. Church bells rang, people cheered, and that night the village was full of joy and laughter. Little did they know that just hours later, the king would slowly rise from his coffin and cackle an evil laugh.

The King no longer needed food or water, no longer needed the basic requirements a human might. His body became consumed by ice, and so did his mind. Over time a thick, white and almost eternal blanket of fog descended on the village, covering it and the castle from sight, as if nature was trying to cover up this horrendous act. The people were confused and scared, not knowing why they had been plunged into cold, why the crops began to fail and why nothing would grow. The King stayed confined to his home, brooding. The land was plunged into an unrelenting winter, only ending in one, short and blissful summer, where the fog lifted, the King retreated into the darkest depths of his home and the children played with delight. The parents, however, could only try to look happy, because they knew that the struggle for food and warmth would come again soon. In one of these parents, our story begins.

21

The winter had been getting harder and harder. Food was scarce; warmth was almost non-existent. This meant for Petrov that he had less and less to feed his children. He was a dark haired, short and strong young man, no different from many others in the village. He had been a child during the King's reign of darkness, and still felt that utter hatred for the looming symbol of tyranny that reigned over the village and the people in it. Every morning he awoke to see the castle; when he worked he had a direct view, and at night he would look through the window and glare at it. He had two children; his fifteen-year-old son Vladimir and his daughter Yelena, who was the same age. He had a wife, Melina. As for everyone else, life was a fight for survival. Every night they had to have the same watery soup, and still they all went to bed hungry, their stomachs growling like chained beasts; meanwhile the King sat happily in his throne, secluded from society. But the next day, everything changed.

It was a normal day. Petrov woke up once again to a cold and dark house. The house was tiny, and was not meant to fit two people, much less four. It had just one storey, and its only rooms were a child's room, Melina and Petrov's room, a kitchen and a cramped bathroom. Water seeped through the walls, making it damp and cold, the children layering extra blankets at night in a desperate attempt to preserve warmth. The garden was small and barren, where all of the plants were long dead. And everyday, as Petrov surveyed all that his gracious King had gifted to him, his hate became ever greater every time he looked upon his starving children, it grew and grew. And that morning, it was ready to explode. But no time for that now. His only priority was food, taking his issues one day at a time. He got up early, threw on his coat and headed out to the road. At that time, the village was virtually empty, a ghost town, the poorly cobbled streets devoid of life. The villagers could not use horses, as they required food. Petrov walked on the eerie streets, his over-sized coat sweeping across the floor.

The walk was long and cold, but finally he arrived. His job was as a blacksmith, making anything from teapots to maces, and he had chosen his forge where he hammered at his work to have a direct view of Bram Castle through the window. And it was this particular day, when he was smashing away fashioning the head of a pike, he looked up. Then down, then up again. It was this moment, in the back of his mind, where the beginnings of a plan began to shape.

All day Petrov could only sculpt the plan in his head, making an excuse that he was sick as to get home and begin to really think about it. The walk he took every day seemed like an eternity, but finally he arrived. He unlocked the door, and in his excitement it fell off its hinges; however, he did not care. All day he thought and thought, working out the finest details in his mind. By the time Melina returned home, he had worked it all out. Melina was a tall, blonde-haired woman who worked as a carpenter. She pushed the broken door open and exclaimed

"What happened to the door!?" Petrov was too excited to take notice of this question, immediately jumping up from his chair, knocking it over as he rushed towards his wife.

"Melina!" he said, through quickening breaths, "I may have figured it out!"

She stared at him, quite confused at this point, lost for words, then managed to say: "Figured out what? Also what happened to the door?"

Petrov paced the living room, unable to contain his excitement. "Never mind the door, but I figured out how to save ourselves! We've been living under this tyrannous monster for too long, and I will not see my children starve in his grasp. I've come up with a plan to rebel against him. I will not watch as more and more perish under his gaze. His time is over. The

23

people's time has come." Melina looked at him blankly.

"Wha-, Wh-, Wh-" she stammered. Then she said sharply, "You better fix the door.".

One week later, Petrov's plan was finally coming into action. It had taken hours to convince Melina, his colleagues and friends to meet in the village hall that night. Petrov had made the walk there with Melina, and when he finally arrived, he stopped, and surveyed the building that stood before him. It was the epitome of what his home had become. It was a small, almost mismatched building which had been thrown together with as little resources as possible, so it leaned to the right and part of the roof had caved in, which had been hastily repaired by covering it with layers of leaves connected by a wooden grid made from sticks collected from the forest floor. It had no windows, as things had become so bad recently that windows could not be replaced, so they broke, one by one until all that remained were square holes in the walls. "This," Petrov thought to himself, "is the best we can do. This is all that we can muster. Through all our trials and tribulation, all our struggles, all we do, this is what we can make." The rage inside of him bubbled, pure hatred, with no sense of rationality left. However, he suppressed this for now. He had to be patient. With a deep breath, he burst into the hall and changed the lives of everyone in it.

As soon as Petrov entered, the chatter and bustle died down, heads turning, whispers and pointing towards the entrance where he had entered. Almost the entire village was there, colleagues, friends, family, strangers. They had all come to see him. Better not make them come for nothing. He wasted no time, striding toward the hastily built elevated stage and surveying the crowd below him. Here he had the chance to change lives. Here he had the chance to make lives. Here he had the chance to save lives. He began to speak, the words coming to him easily, as if he'd rehearsed them a million times.

"We live under a regime so tyrannous and evil that we have forgotten what food and warmth are like. How many have died from the cold? Starvation? Building collapse? I say too many. I say we've been living like this too long!" Nods of agreement shifted through the crowd, and Petrov was just getting started. "Things don't have to be like this. We don't have to live like this. I dream of a world where people live happy lives, always kept warm and dry. I dream of a world where every night you know what will be on your plate the next!" The crowd was very invested now. Almost everyone was nodding, and there were some cheers. "I dream of a world where we don't have an eternal winter, where we don't worry about our families, where our buildings are built like fortresses! Change is inevitable! Change has come!" Everyone was cheering him now. Hats were being thrown up, and in every face he saw something you don't see often in the village. Hope.

The people began to arm themselves, supplied by Petrov and his fellow blacksmiths. Armour, swords, shields, battle axes, all were being pumped out at a massive rate.
While Petrov was supplying weapons to all the people willing to fight for freedom, the next in line astonished him. "Valdmir?! Yelena!? What are you doing?" The two children stood before him, their eyes shining with the same rage that Petrov saw in himself. Seeing it in them seemed... wrong. They had Melina's blonde hair, but Petrov's short and strong build. Both were wearing the same long, threadbare overcoat.

"We have to fight dad," Vladimir insisted

"We're old enough" Yelena argued, "Now we know you'll sa-"

25

"Absolutely not. I am not letting my own children risk their lives, no matt-"

"But we're fifteen!" she demanded, throwing her hands around to emphasise the point.

"Thank you, Yelena, I knew you'd see sense eventually."

"That's not what she meant!" Vladimir protested, almost shouting his words. People were staring at them now, watching the entire argument take place.

"I will have no further argument. You will not fight. I am not putting you anywhere where there is a one percent chance that you will be even necessarily hurt, I will never send you out there. Now go home." The last words were delivered with such massive force and authority that the two physically stepped back. Finally, they trudged home, their mission a failure. Petrov cast a sad glance toward them, and then returned to his work.

The day had finally come. A force of about a hundred men and women gathered by the village gates, each carrying the weapon they had chosen. Maces, swords, spears, battle-axes, bows, every weapon someone could think of was being used. Petrov himself was wielding a pike, which had given him the idea to rise up in the first place. Every person to enlist were given armour, some had chest plates, many had helmets and gauntlets, though there were some who had no armour at all. They had all rallied here to fight for their freedom. Petrov found an elevated bit of land and spoke to the villagers who had come. He cleared his throat and began to speak:

"Hello all of you who have so bravely come to fight for your family, your friends, your village. Today we change lives, today we change history. We shall show the king that we will not cower or whimper, that we can and will fight for our lives. Let's fight for our freedom." There were cheers from all the villagers, and Petrov jumped down from the hill he was at and got to walking. They trudged along, and finally they got close. They had arrived.

The villagers neared the symbol of the tyranny that had towered over them all these cold and unforgiving years. The same deep white fog that had dominated their village hung around the crumbling towers as if unable to let go. The battlements were falling, and almost all of the east side of the castle had a thick green moss creeping up the walls. No windows were lighted, and if there were any life to be found in the dark corridors of the castle, no sign was given of it. The moat surrounding it, like the rest of large bodies of water in the village, was frozen over in a thick sheet of ice, topped with a blanket of snow. They put themselves into a formation where all flanks where defended, with spears and swords pointed in every direction. Finally, they reached the drawbridge, which was raised, stopping them from approaching. Questions began to be raised

"What do we do?"

"Is this the end?"

"Should we turn back?"

Suddenly, the drawbridge slammed down, as if pushed by a giant hand, therefore opening the way for the villagers to enter. The way was clear, but nobody seemed inclined to actually go in. Except for one man. Petrov strode onto the bridge, jumped up and down testing its stability, then gestured for the others to follow suit. With a wary look at each other, the villagers crossed, one by one until everyone was standing before the great stone entrance to Bram Castle. And one by one, they entered.

As they entered, gasps shimmered through the crowd, the villagers not believing what they were seeing. The castle had once been full of warmth and fire, but now it was filled with the freezing of ice. It was everywhere, the floor had a slippery layer of it over the top, the carpet had frost everywhere on it, so that when you stepped it made a loud crunching noise and the chandeliers had long icicles hanging from them, some almost touching the floor itself. The thick mist that had blanketed them for years had flooded into the castle, meaning they could not see to the end of the corridor. Petrov and the villagers had entered into a massive hall, which they could just barely see to the end of. Lined along the wall of the hall were ice warriors, each carrying a different frozen weapon, and by each of them was a large, Greek-style column . What the villagers saw at the end of the hall shocked them. A throne, and on it, the shape of a man.

"He is here," Petrov muttered, and, without fear or thought, began to approach.

Petrov strode toward the man on the throne, the villagers warily following suit. Finally, after a short walk that seemed to last a thousand years, Petrov halted, and to a sharp inhale of breath, this action was soon followed by all the villagers. The old man on the throne had a large beard that dropped all the way down to his lap and he had a big, round face with little tufts of hair. He was wearing a long, deep blue robe that swept past his feet, and had a crown studded with light blue sapphires. The odd thing about him was that he was... icy. His beard seemed to be made of frost and it was the same story with his robe, crunching as he moved. Icicles clung to his chin, his robe, his crown. He lifted a bony finger, and proceeded to croak out in a raspy voice "Why? Why are you here?"

Petrov seemed stunned for a moment, then caught himself and stammered out, "We- we've come to kill you." The king stared

28

at Petrov with his cold, unforgiving eyes. Then he burst out laughing, wheezing for breath as he slapped his hands up and down on his throne.

"Kill me! Kill me! Ha! Oh, you villagers do make me laugh." He continued to move into a fit of wheezing laughter. "Boy, I don't think you know who I am. Have you come to the wrong castle?" Then he carried on his raspy laugh. The villagers looked at each other all very confused, some wondering if they really did have the wrong castle. Petrov, however, didn't think that, and he charged up toward the King, pushing his pike ahead of him and letting loose a guttural scream. The King continued to laugh, then flicked his hand in the way toward him. Petrov was flung into the wall by a massive gust of wind, slamming into one of the columns, cracking that side in the process. The villagers all took a step back, except for two, who took a couple steps forward, then took off their helmets, revealing the two raging faces of Yelena and Vladmir. The pair approached, rousing the villagers in the process, and causing them all to advance with them.

The King didn't seem to care, continuing to laugh and laugh. Suddenly he stopped, and spoke to them, his tone serious. "Do you really think that you can just kill me? You think I don't have protection? Guards!" He called, and every ice sculpture carrying weapons stepped out from by the columns and began to attack. The sculpture's limbs grinded against their bodies, creaking as they slowly moved arms and hands to raise their weapons, and, with massive force, slammed their weapons into the villagers.

"Don't just stand there!" Vladmir cried, "Fight!" With this rally, villagers began to attack, slicing into the warriors of ice. But every time they made a connection, their swords simply stuck to the ice like glue, and when they tried to let go, frost would travel down their weapon, stabbing their hand allowing the warriors to decimate. Vladimir and Yelena were fighting side by side, but they realised early on that attacking would result in death, so they only blocked attacks, until Yelena had an idea. She grabbed one of the ice soldiers' weapons, meaning that frost trapped her hand there, but all that did was mean that she could take it. She yanked it away from the sculpture carrying it and used it jab at the limbs. These limbs began to crack and fall apart, and finally just the chest and head were left, and they fell to the floor, shattering. Vladimir soon caught on to this idea, and so did the other villagers. Finally, with their numbers substantially lessened, the villagers destroyed the last ice sculpture. Then they turned toward the king.

Petrov had never felt such massive, searing pain. It was like someone had thrown him into a vat of lava, yanked him out again, then thrown him into a frozen lake. He couldn't remember where he was, which made him extremely confused and disoriented. Where was he? Who were the large group of people over there and why did they have weapons? Two of them were standing in front of the group, approaching a man on a throne. They looked... familiar, like he knew them, knew what they were like. One, a short, blonde haired boy, turned toward him, and though Petrov couldn't read lips very well, he thought the boy said, "Dad." It all flooded back to him now, all the memories of his friends, family and his children. All the rage exploded within him, all the suffering. Now, the King who had caused all of that, was approaching his own children. He stumbled to his feet, almost falling over in the process, but he did regain balance. He picked up his pike and charged, pummelling it straight into the King's side. This time he wasn't expecting it. From the wound, instead of blood, ice spread from the wound to the King's body. Finally, it closed over his face and feet, and after a second, the ice King fell to the floor, shattering him and the tyranny he had caused. It was silent for a moment, until the entire room burst into cheering.

One year later...

Petrov surveyed his kingdom of ice, and the people who served him in it. It had been a year since he lifted that crown to his head, since he became winter. He had forgotten long ago what it was like to be starving, how it felt to watch children huddle up for warmth in blankets. Vladimir, Yelena and Melina were safely locked away in a tower, unable to nag him about morals and goodness anymore. And as he surveyed his kingdom, he began to laugh.

A Warm Tale for Cold Weather
by Hugh Jezzard

Winter has arrived as it always does. The cold invaded the lands, forcing the heat to shelter in the fires of men and women. Snow wiped the colour out of the surrounding lands.

While the winter takes its toll on the lands, let us allow the story to begin.

In a valley covered in snow there sat a cobble-stoned courtyard in front of a wooden house with a thatched roof. A husband and wife were sitting inside, watching their firewood turn to embers while the sound of the wind howled outside. The whistling of the kettle broke the silence. The wife got up, went to the kettle, picked it up with a hint of urgency. She turned and looked with pity at a badger that was wounded. A cut still showing fresh blood trickling down, a face crusted in snow. Slowly the wife poured the hot water on a piece of cloth and gently padded it on the badger's wound, while the husband prepared the supper for the badger. The badger, which was eager for supper, smelt it with happiness. The husband walked towards the badger and gently poured the food into the badger's mouth allowing the badger to swallow. The daily treatment for the injured badger was over. The wife and husband went to bed listening to the howling of the wind and the crackling of the fire. The sound of the creaking rafters slowly subsided into nothing.

The sun shot hopeful rays through the windows of the wooden, thatched house. Husband and wife awoke to the realisation that they needed to get firewood and search for injured animals. They opened the door and were greeted by cold, icy air and the weak light from a midwinter sun, ever failing to repel the winter.

The crunching of the snow under their boots followed them as they made their way through the wooded valley.

Deciding to separate, the wife watched as her husband started collecting the essential wood for their hungry fire. He would plant more trees later that spring. She turned and trekked, searching for signs of distressed animals: unusual trails in the snow, drops of dried blood, broken branches. She thankfully found none. Instead she spotted, through the snow, some plants she could use for healing, and gathered those eagerly, stuffing them inside her warm coat.

She headed back to the house, terribly aware of the sun fading and the strong need to get home before dark.

She opened the door and her husband greeted her thankfully with a mug of warm tea. He looked concerned but said nothing. Working together, they treated the badger that was now healing well. It was dark by now and the wind was howling vigorously like a pack of wolves. The couple moved around the kitchen, lighting candles and fastening doors and windows securely. They decided to go to bed to sleep out the advancing storm.

They woke up. The sound of howling wind was joined by the sound of snow hitting the house, rattling the rafters. Slightly muffled, they heard the sound of a distressed animal. They put on their heavy coats and boots, opened the door against the strong, cold wind, and slipped through.

They could see nothing but a void of white. The blizzard was vicious and deadly but they had no choice. They had to find the animal to make up for their past. It was their mission. It would always be their life.

The couple wrestled their way through dense snow and against strong wind, still hearing the distant whine of a wounded animal.

The sound of cracking filled the air and a dark shape started falling towards them. The husband stumbled. A majestic fir tree fell to the ground like a noble soldier falling in battle. The husband rolled to avoid the main trunk, missed his footing and his body weight dragged him down a steep, snowy hillside dotted with shrubs and saplings. The sound of crackling soon followed.

He regained his breath and called through the whirling snowflakes to his wife that she should keep tracking the animal. He could survive, it might not.

In the worsening storm, the wife trudged on making painstakingly slow progress against the power of nature. Without doubt the animal cries increased in volume and distress. It was a sickening cry, filled with pain and desperation. She increased her pace, trying to reach the wounded creature. And there was a brown outline in the blizzard of snowflakes. It was a large animal, bigger than her, but she didn't hesitate. Reaching for its warmth, her hands encountered blood. The animal was wounded and frightened and needed comfort, rest and treatment. It was a young male elk with a gaping wound on its shoulder where a broken branch had embedded itself. Blood was gushing out of the shoulder; the wound was fresh. Using her scarf as a bandage, she bound the wound and then led the elk, slowly, back to the house where the stable would give it shelter and a place to rest.

Out of the howling wind, the stable smelt of cow, horse and hay. There were soft noises as the cow and horse breathed and rustled in their grassy bedding. The wild elk was not used to domestic animals or a stable but was too weak to pull away. The wife soothed him with her gentle hands and, in lantern light, tended to his wounds, placed oats and water nearby, and settled the frightened animal for the night.

Returning to the cottage, a branch snapped. The sound startled her. But it was only her husband who had returned.

Looking into the elk's eyes, the old man remembered a time when he killed animals for sport. He had been proud to take the lives of innocent creatures until that day when, creeping towards an elk with his hands on the sword's handle, he was ready to slice. But the sword remained in its scabbard because when he was ready to swing at the elk, it looked into his eyes and he saw his past and saw how stupid he was to kill animals and he dropped to the ground crying.

Slowly, the husband returned to the present, sad, but happy that he had changed.

The rest of the winter was spent in the daily round of seeking and healing the injured animals of the North Forest, making amends for years of cruelty and killing.

When spring came, the badger was fully recovered, her cut was a memory and her fur shone with health. The young elk had also made a full recovery. In the ever-strengthening sunlight of a new season the couple watched the animals take their first steps back into the forest. Life began again as it always does, like a new year filled with hope.

Let us now end the story and watch winter come and, one day, end. The cycle of the seasons. We live with nature.

Imagine Your Own by Jooha Park

Another year passes. The winter snow floats down onto the red rooftops of the village. The merry carols drifted out of the brick chimneys to a far away wood where imaginations come true...

"AND STAY OUT!!!"

A fiery voice breaks the lovely music and birds fly away from their perches. The door shuts and a lonely girl sits on the porch. She sighs as she fiddles with her name tag for the Christmas choir. It read:

SONYA WOODSTOCK

Sonya stares up and watches her white breath disappear into the starry sky. Her nose becomes numb, and she decides to walk home. The long way through the forest.
The soft snow crunches as Sonya drags her cold body through the dark forest. She arrives at her cabin and shakes the small bell.

RING RING RING

Inside the house, two fluffy ears perch up and, with monstrous legs, pound all the way to where the bell calls. A grey, little mouth opens and barks. The door creaks open as a small husky emerges from the warm cabin house.

"Yes, I'm back. Were you good?"

The dog barks back with glee and bounces next to Sonya as she tries to get a mug of cocoa. She sits down into her fiery red armchair and begins to open the pages of her magical world.

37

A flip of a page and Sonya was running away from *Baba Yaga* and her *house with chicken legs.* A flip of another and she's dancing around with the prince from *Cinderella.* Her adventures go past in a blur, stealing for the poor with *Robin Hood,* being suspicious of the wolf in *Red Riding Hood* and helping the youngest pig help make his house in *Three Little Pigs.*

But Sonya's favourite adventure is her own, where she is playing tag in a meadow with her family, where she is scoffing tarts on a picnic blanket and where she actually feels like home. But alas, poor Sonya, she has no family and is suffering from the freezing cold this winter...

This story was Sonya's. But could it be yours?

A Winter Story by Iris Pittard

'Twas the night before Christmas' wrote 10 year old Lucy from the comfort of her wardrobe. Snow was fluttering softly against the window of her bedroom, gently tapping to come in. Curls of wind slid in through the cracks in the window frame, twisting their way the doors of her wardrobe, and Lucy shivered. She wrapped her knitted blanket round her tightly, and continued writing. Her in steady hands moved slowly across the page, writing, 'and all through the house, not a creature was stirring, not even a-' She paused and frowned, trying to remember the last word of the Christmas rhyme. In the end she scratched out the sentence, and began again. 'The house was still, like-' she stopped and thought, then looked at her alarm clock on one of the many wooden shelves along the left hand side of her wardrobe. It was nine o'clock on Christmas Eve, and she was meant to be in bed. She gathered up her Christmas cards for her mother and father, and tucked them away in her sock drawer, then hopped into bed. A loud whistling gale filled her bedroom, and it swept under her blanket, chilling her feet. Lucy pulled the covers over her a bit more, and stared at the ceiling. Dangling fairies met her eyes, poorly sewn, but they still had the shape of the wings and the flowing dress. She turned the other way, then breathed heavily in and out, until her eyes could take it no longer, and closed.

She was standing in a large garden, with towering walls made of brightly coloured paper, decorated with lines of Christmas trees and Santa's jolly red face, bells hanging from mistletoe, and wreaths of holly and ivy, topped with a blanket of snow. There were many shimmery spheres of blue and pink littered all over the garden, Lucy got curious. She bent down, and picked up what looked like a flower petal, only it wasn't a flower petal, but was a small, wing-like shape, which looked like it was made of thin plastic. Hanging off the wing was a small creature, with arms as thin as twigs, and a face no bigger than a thumbnail. It wore a blue dress which was made from satin, and it had dainty feet, which slid into crystal shoes. Lucy studied the creature's face for a moment, then let it fall out of her hand, as a trail of blood began to leak from its mouth. She shuddered, repulsed, and continued to walk into the garden. Jingling bells echoed throughout the garden, but they seemed more clangy than any usual bells she had heard. She began to look for an exit, starting to get a creeping sensation that this Christmas-like garden was not as it seemed. All around her she could see buzzing sort of things, almost like bees, tending to, what it looked like to be, miniature Christmas trees.

"But you're not bees- Why- you're fairies!" Lucy gasped, as one of them flew into her hand. An image of the dead creature she had dropped moments before flashed into her mind. Lucy shuddered. She then stared at the fairy in her palm. Her pinkish skirts billowed in the breeze, and her flowing golden hair was twisted in an intricate plait behind her. But something about her was not quite right, thought Lucy. Snow began to fall softly on the ground now, and several flakes dissolved on the back of her dressing gown, making her shiver. Lucy looked at the fairy again. She had a pale grey tinge to her flawless complexion, and her eyes seemed sullen and dull. Lucy thought for a minute, and then spoke to the fairy.

"Dear Fairy, may I ask if you are ok? You do not seem at all well." The fairy did not reply, so Lucy bent down closer to her palm to be closer to her, and repeated.

"Fairy, are you sick?" Suddenly the loud noise of beating wings stopped. Lucy got up and looked around the garden. All of the fairies who had been working had stopped flying and were gently hovering all around. They were all directed to her, but their eyes had rolled back into their heads, showing off their milky-white eyeballs. She looked down at the fairy next to her, but she too had gone all funny. Wherever she went, their eyes followed her. Then they all chanted as one:

'Twas the night before Christmas, and all through the house,
Not a creature was stirring, not even a mouse.

But Jane here has awoken now, and she is restless,
For annoy her now, and your life won't be endless.
She sits under needles, hidden but there,
Now she knows you're alive, you have to be aware.
Avoid her, and remember, don't go down the stair,
She is waiting for you, and don't go into her lair,
Jane wants you, Lucy Brown,
Watch out for her tune; that means she's around... "

The fairies stopped chanting, and they all looked at Lucy one
more time. Then, in a raspy voice, the fairy next to her croaked:
"S-s-she cont-trol. B-b-beware."

DONG. DONG. DONG.
Lucy woke up her eyes flying open.
DONG. DONG.
She looked around her, gasping for breath.
DONG. DONG. DONG.
She stared up at her ceiling.
DONG. DONG.
All her fairies were gone.
DONG.
The sound of the church bells stopped. It was officially
midnight.
Lucy took a second to think everything through. She decided
that her dream was most certainly not related to anything in real
life, but how could she be sure? The snow was still falling
heavily outside, and the chill still crept in through the window
crack, but something had changed. Her room was still the same,
her writing desk was as tidy as it usually was, and her clothes
had been picked off her bedroom floor. But everything was too
silent. Not even the gale made any noise. And then the tune
started.
"Ring a ring a roses,
You will fall to me,
Under the Christmas tree,

41

Large and square, that's me,
Colours of bunting by the fireplace,
It will say your name,
You are mine Lucy Brown,
And you will come to me again,
Atishoo, Atishoo We all fall down"
It was faint, but you could still hear it, echoing downstairs, past
the coat rack, through the kitchen, and into the nursery, where
the-
"Christmas tree is." whispered Lucy.

Lucy stood there in her dressing gown, shaking. She forcefully
told herself that it wasn't real- it was all just a bad dream, though
something told her that you can only wake up once. She
opened the door to her room and stepped out into the landing.
The tune hung in the air, the chants getting louder as her feet
padded on the carpet at the top of the stairs. The top stair was
always creaky, she took care to skip that one, and hurried down
the rest of the stairs. The nursery was at the very end of the hall,
shrouded in darkness, and Lucy fumbled for the light switch for
the hall. The lights flickered, and then turned off, Lucy flicked
the switch once, twice, three times, but the lights would still not
turn on. Jane wanted her to arrive in darkness. If she was even
there. Walking down to the nursery door felt much more
different than it usually did. Perhaps it was because it was
Christmas, or that it was dark, but there was something that
made everything seem less and less like a bad dream, the more
she walked towards the room at the end of the corridor. The
lights were flickering in the nursery, and suddenly music began
to play, filling the corridor with a haunting sensation. Lucy
reached the room. Heart pounding, her fingers stretched
towards the doorknob. She pushed it. It swung open.

The room was set out perfectly. The lights were tangled down
by the fireplace and around the Christmas tree, the decorations
were hung from the branches, and crackly Christmas music was

playing from the stereo in the corner. Lucy's breath gently slowed. There was nothing. She was just imagining everything. But as she turned to go out the door, the tune started up again.
"Ring a ring a roses,
You will fall to me,
Under the Christmas tree-"
Lucy did not imagine that. She began to shake. The sound was coming from under the Christmas tree.
"Under the Christmas tree," stuttered Lucy. Her eyes searched the presents.
"Large and square, that's me," the tune continued. Lucy stared at a large, shoebox-shaped present.
"Colours of bunting by the fireplace," it sang. Lucy looked at the present, covered in red and green wrapping paper. Then she looked at the red and green bunting by the fireplace.
"It will say your name,". Lucy looked at the label.
"To Lucy. From Jane." she whispered.
"You are mine, Lucy Brown
And you will come to me again
Attishoo, Attishoo,
We all fall down," sang the box. The last note hung in the air. Lucy grabbed the present. She ripped open the paper and turned the present around. The doll inside had curly golden-brown hair, a white nightie, and a cream-coloured dressing gown. Lucy looked at her cream dressing gown and her white nightie. The doll stared up at her.
"Just a toy, just a toy," whispered Lucy. As she placed the box down under the Christmas tree, the doll blinked. It blinked again. A wave of terror fell over Lucy. It felt like her stomach had just dropped. Then the mouth smiled, showing off its overly-white teeth.
"Hello, Lucy Brown," said Jane.

The Packa by Benjamin Tomlinson

Was that something in the night? A growling from above?
Looking up, Slobber saw a faint shape looking down on him
through the cold night air. A friend or foe? It jumped down,
dashing towards him at an extremely fast pace, skidding over the
slightly frosty ground. With a sickening crunch as it made
impact, Slobber was knocked backward off his feet, exploding
in a flurry of barking and ripping into the invader. Slamming
them swiftly across the ground, leaping onto them, crashing
onto bare earth, turning around, banging against the wall,
making his way up, still fighting, dizzy, sight blurred, falling. It
was over. Just like that.

Waking up, blinking open his eyes, finding himself on the
bare cold floor, wincing as he tried to get up, remembering the
fight last night. But why? He held almost no grudges against any
of the major packs, careful to avoid their patch, even if it meant
going hungry for several nights until finding a good meal. Why
didn't he join one? Simple. Having to follow orders, always
having to stay alert for enemies. Maybe he would have to join
one now. A tactical recruit form a pack? Forcing him to join
them? Unlikely. Then why, WHY him? What did he do?
Thinking back across his short memory, wondering. Yesterday.
Sun-high. He was searching through a dumpster. Another dog
came. Not a dog he knew. His little hunting patch that strange
dog was on. His little patch. Slobber's patch. Slobber then
drove off. Maybe a bad idea. Might need to join a pack soon.
These thoughts fired through his small pea-sized head, until he
came to a conclusion. He would create his own pack. The
Packa.

Days later, and Slobber was out patrolling the slightly bigger
patch of the Packa. Growler, Chaser and Flower had joined the
group. Growler and Flower were siblings. Chaser was a personal
old friend of Slobber (even though Slobber wasn't that old).

Slobber was determined to keep him and his friends safe, against any dangers that may face them in the future. It was another cold night. He shivered. Hearing a noise above his head, fearing the worst, he glanced up, prodding Chaser as he did so. He saw the same dog that attacked him, standing up on a house with ease. Before Slobber could react, the dog was gone, fleeing, but Slobber knew they would be back. With more...

The following days were hard. It was starting to freeze, and with it, everything got colder, the days shorter, the nights longer. The Packa didn't do much as a result, only travelling around to get food, and do patrols. They did grow though. Two little scrawny dogs came, pleading for a place to stay, and Slobber hoped more like them would come, seeking the safety, warmth and good meals that the pack brought. And only hours later, a dog came, not little nor scrawny like the others, but strong looking, well fed and having a strange air about them. They walked as though they were in charge, not flinching a bit even though multiple enemies outflanked them on every side, blocking their exit. They almost ignored all the other dogs, coming straight to Slobber, and bowing down, much to Slobber's surprise as shown on his face.

"Oh great lord of this small yet prosperous land." flattered the dog. "I have come to give you a proposition from my great and wholesome leader. I, we, think all sides will benefit from this most fair and brilliant deal. It is simple. You disband your pack, and join us, the BigPACK, and help us grow ever so much more rich, and successful. The choice is yours." stepping back, out of earshot, granting the Packa enough privacy to make this life changing, but seemingly simple decision.

"So... Um - Are you going to decide for us?" asked Flower.

"No, we're going to have a vote." Slobber replied surely, yet remained uncertain whether the odds would be in his favour. "If you would like to keep the pack intact, go to the bin shed. And... if you want to disband the group and either join the

BigPACK, or just leave and become without a pack, go to the sleeping spot."

He waited in intense silence, as slowly all the members started shuffling round him. Chaser went straight to the bin shed. Growler and Flower put their heads together and started talking in short hushed barks. The two little scrawny dogs shuffled nervously in the middle, seemingly not really sure whether they should have an opinion in a matter like this after joining only recently. Slobber stood in the same place, waiting until all of his pack had voted.

Coming up to him, one of the scrawny dogs asked, "Should we vote? After all, we have only been in the pack for a short time..." trailing off, looking down at the floor and shuffling their paws.

"The future of the Packa will be yours too. Vote, and let us see the results." Slobber replied, getting more and more nervous as the time passed.

What was taking Growler and Flower so long? Didn't they want the Packa? Looking over at them, seeing them nearly shouting at each other, then seeing Growler race off to the bin shed, while surprisingly Flower went to the sleeping spot, with the two scrawny dogs following. Slobber joined Growler and Chaser, the vote clear but undecidable. Who would make the final decision? Before anything could be said, Growler glanced apologetically at Slobber, and bounded over to join Flower. So it was decided. Slobber was breaking up the Packa, and joining the suspicious BigPACK, or would be left out, alone again and in the freezing cold as winter was nearly at its worst...

The Winter Cold by Benjamin Tomlinson

He shivered. The cold winds seeped through his woolly
jumper, and their freezing fingers slid down his spine. His snow
boots were loosely fitted around his feet, while his hat was no
more than a rag. And his pants were no better. They stretched
down his legs, yet stopped three quarters to his grimy feet. 'Hey
Ethan!'. He heard a shout from a distance, and turned in that
direction.

'You're late,' he spoke in a quiet voice, almost a whisper, but
with much meaning to it.

'So? Does it matter at all?' the girl replied. She was much
better dressed than Ethan. She had a warm coat, fitting trousers,
sparkly boots and even a scarf. She made quick distance of the
snow and ran up to Ethan, then past him, heading into a forest.
Ethan followed, stepping in the freshly made tracks she left
behind. As they entered the forest, the girl slowed her pace,
letting Ethan catch up to her, whilst looking around at the trees,
stripped bare of their leaves, barely clinging to existence.

'Where are we going today Melva?' Ethan asked, already up
half a tree, then out of sight.

'Wait up, I found somewhere new today!' Melva shouted
back, also disappearing out of sight into and up a tree.

Melva dropped down, Ethan followed, they were exhausted.
They had gone to the new place Melva had found. And as they
departed, Melva melting slowly into the snow, Ethan felt lonely
yet again. He plodded home, lifting one drowsy foot after the
other. And as the wind picked up, and more snow came piling
out of the sky, his pace neither faltered nor quickened. As he
got home, he opened the door of the house, letting a chilly and
icy wind gust through the door, rushing to meet warmer, stale
air inside. This probably alerted his Uncle, for in a few seconds,
he was being rushed inside, and scolded. Left on a step, Ethan
got up and made his way to his bedroom, slamming the door
behind him, with such force that it was heard throughout the
whole of the small household.

Melva walked out of her house, stretching in the bright morning sunshine. It wasn't yet spring, but some excited green shoots were already breaking through the snow and into the open. It was a fresh new day and Melva wanted to explore. But obviously, not alone. With her dog yapping, and Melva running, they made a lot of noise. Bursting through trees which hadn't yet shaken off the snow, and making new tracks deeply imprinted into the snow, it was a fun time. Panting, arriving home, sweaty yet smiling, she plunged into the living room. She didn't want the weekend to be over, but it was going to be soon.

Ethan searched for his pen. He was sure it was somewhere in his bag. He checked everywhere, even his lunch bag! He couldn't find it.

"Having trouble?" Micheal asked, holding up three, no four pens, and throwing them around.

"Please." Ethan asked.

"No, don't." jeered Clont. Micheal was pretending to decide, putting one in his mouth, pretending to chew on it.

"Fine," he finally replied holding a pen out, "but, on one condition. You give me the answer to the extension activity for English."

"But, I didn't figure that one out myself." Ethan stammered, "Wasn't that an extension? It isn't mandatory."

"OK," Micheal replied. He held his hand down and walked off with Clont. Ethan looked on as Micheal walked away, whispering something to Clont as they walked along. They both laughed, Clont glancing back at Ethan. They were even talking about him! He fumed. Stomping off to class, likely to get a C3, he saw Melva. He ran up to her.

"Can I have a pen?" he asked, knowing this would be his only chance to get a pen. Melva didn't put a pen in her mouth, chew it or pretend to take long to decide. Instead she simply took a spare pen out of her bag, and handed it to Ethan.

"Give it back at the end of the day." she replied. "Oh, and don't forget to bring your own tomorrow!" she shouted back, walking to her next lesson. Ethan smiled, taking the pen to his next lesson.

Melva unpacked her bag, and got out her homework. There were three pieces of paper, and five books. It had been a busy day. She placed them in a corner, hoping she wouldn't forget them, and sat down. She turned on the TV - got bored. She started to read a book - got bored. She started a wordsearch - didn't find one word, and got bored. She even went outside to look around - got bored. She didn't know what to do. Everything she tried to do was boring. Then she got a text from Alex;

yo wassup! u wanna come 2 my house 2day?? i am getting a new phone. i am gonna do lots of cool things. COME OVER AND PARTY!!! bring ur peeps. all of dem welcome!!!!

She knew what to do. She got up, out of her house and went to Alex's. She knocked on the door, and a huge outblast of music, warm air, shouts, and screams came from inside. The door was flung open, and Alex was standing at the door.
"Come In!!!" she shouted, whooping loudly, and whoops sounded further in, as if in response. Melva hopped into the mess, partying and having a bunch of fun. She got out late into the night, staggering to and fro. But all in all she had a good day. A great day.

Ethan blinked sleep from his wary eyes. He didn't want to get up, but he knew he would have to. He got out of bed, brushed his teeth, ate his breakfast, and put on his adventuring outfit; a set of rags and clothes, which might not have looked like much, but they had shared some of his fondest memories...

Melva woke up, yawning. She fumbled for her phone, which was hanging precariously off the edge of her desk, she grabbed it, then turned it on whilst blinking her eyes awake. She looked at the time: 8:49. Then a message popped up underneath.

'Where are you? Ethan.'

What? She thought, checking the date. Oh. She realised. She was going to meet Ethan at the clearing! And she'd forgotten! She grabbed her outdoor clothes, threw them on, grabbed a bag, filled it with some snacks and essentials, and rushed out of the front door, shutting it with a bang. She ran, half slipping, half sliding on the ice/snow. She arrived at the start of the woods, panting, and continued forward, ever so often checking the time. She was nearly there. She panted as she ran through the woods at a faster pace, trees, bushes, and branches flashing past her like a blur. Then something tugged on her leg. She fell on the ground hard, face splat on the frozen dirt, the contents of her bag spilling out onto the floor like a messy painting, her leg in pain. She screamed, but the only reply was a squirrel disturbing leaves as it rushed off, and a bird shrieking an alarming cry, and flapping its wings, heading off into the sky. She turned slowly around, every part of her body shrieking at her to stop. She saw a barbed wire near the floor, with part of her jeans on it, but not only that, it had remains of a fox, a mouse tail, and a few feathers. Melva looked on, horrified, and tried to scramble away, only to see a shadow looming in behind her...

Ethan paced around. The last message he had received from Melva was half an hour ago. She should be here by now. Maybe something was wrong? But he didn't know, should he go and check and possibly make Melva search for him or should he wait but possibly put Melva in more danger? He headed out, jumping over wilting nettles, and clearing fallen trees. He stomped on the remains of leaves, hearing satisfying crunching, and headed towards the edge of the forest.

Melva woke up. She could hear murmurs around her, and scrambled to her feet, only to collapse and gasp in pain as the leg she had injured had clearly not recovered a single bit.

Faces turned towards her, and one said in a strange accent, "The prisoner is awake!" They scrambled over, opening the cage and bundling her out.

"How much do you think she will sell for?" one asked.

"I bet her family will want her back!" jeered another.

"She might sell well, if we make the right choices." one thoughtfully replied.

"Pah! Just ship her away as a slave somewhere else, people will catch us if she is sold here."

"No! We can keep her to be our slave!"

"I want the profits, she doesn't look fit enough!"

"And she mustn't be smart to fall into our trap!"

"ENOUGH!" Shouted an old, but battle weary looking leader, and all went silent, as he slowly walked towards the trembling Melva. "What is your name?" he asked her, more gentle than he sounded at first, but Melva was still suspicious.

"M-my name is M-Mia." she stumbled out, pretending to be timid and shy. "Can you n-not harm me p-please?"

"Oh, don't worry, we won't harm you, that is unless your parents don't want to buy you back for a reasonable price." said the leader of this group. "Now, where do you live so we can bring you back home?"

"I d-don't know." Melva replied, maybe a bit too stubbornly, for one of the bandits picked her up by the collar of her top, and threw her on the floor.

"I will repeat again Mia, where do you live?" the leader asked through clenched teeth.

"I'll show you." Melva submitted to them.

Ethan stumbled, panting. He didn't stop though. He kept on running, startling sleepy squirrels and frightened mice. Nearly giving up hope, he slowed down, stopping straight in his tracks when he thought he heard Melva? He crept in that direction, trying to not disturb any ground underfoot. As he peered through the branches of a tree, looking into a clearing, filled with... well filled with some dangerous looking people, but most importantly of all, Melva, in the middle of them all. What should he do? Going rushing in to help would most likely get him caught - there were much more of them than there were of him, and they looked much tougher. If he left and came back later, but with the police, it would be better, but the people might be gone. He could try and make a distraction though, and lead the presumed bandits away for long enough to free Melva. That might just work. But what? Rustling in the bushes? Screaming from far away? Melva's parent's coming to find her? Maybe the last one. If he could imitate people calling for Melva... but it might not work. The bandits might get spooked, and run away further. What about a little kid lost in the woods, calling for help? It could work. They caught Melva after all, right? That was it. Ok. So Ethan would run to a place not far from the camp, but far enough away to lead the bandits away for a long time. What about that tall, twisted looking tree that was not that far from this place, but high enough he could possibly get back here quickly. He started putting long, thick tendrils of vines, sometimes intertwined with each other, from tree to tree, making it easy to slide from one to another, making it a quick way to the camp once he set his decoy. Also, if the bandits were to come the same way he was going back, they wouldn't see him in the shelter of the trees! Setting it up took lots of effort and work, but when it was done, he was ready to save Melva from whoever these evil people were.

Melva heard a scream in the woods, then rushing and shouting, at what she presumed were the bandits getting ready for a capture. Poor soul. They would be separated and taken

54

away from their family. At least she could talk to them. Maybe devise a plan to escape. Later, she heard shuffling footsteps outside her cell. It was a little place, made out of makeshift bits and bobs, and thinking about it, it could be easy to break free from. Anyway, Melva's thinking was brought to a close as she heard the footsteps again but louder. Suddenly, light burst into the room, lighting it up nicely for Melva, as there were no windows in her cell. "Melva!" cried a voice from outside. "Come here! Quick! Hush!" Melva was baffled. She hadn't told the bandits her real name. Why were they speaking like that? Then, she noticed Ethan at the door, urging her forward with his hands, making signs to be quiet, and move quickly. Melva scrambled forward, Ethan pushing her out, and out into the forest. She was unsteady on her feet, scrambling to and fro, vision blurring violently as she crashed into a tree. CRASH!!! Shouting came from the camp. "Dang it!" whispered Ethan, shoving Melva up a tree, into a lower branch, Melva was wishing, hoping, she didn't fall. The rest was a blur. She could remember the bandits missing her as they rushed by, Ethan half carrying her home. Warmth, rest, sleep...

Ethan flopped onto the cold mattress, thinking about the day's adventures. He was happy he could be a hero. But sleepy too. Pulling the bedsheet up, and drifting off into a comforting sleep...

Rauður snjór by Freddie Mann

The snow swallowed all sound, all creeks and noise not letting anything travel or move. It was quiet, so quiet even though it felt loud. I moved on through the brush and trees, leaving a path blood drops and the footprints of my leather boots, which were flooding with snow, freezing my feet to a cold like no other. My axe left a trail like that of a snake, giving slight waves in its direction. The dragging made a sound like a blunt knife on stone, the scraping confirming that there was something under the snow. Left behind me were the souls of my enemies and friends, the memories of my and my comrades crossing the whale road felt like old sagas weaved by the Norns, I felt like my saga was about to wrap up. It was the last week of Ýlir midway through Yule, I choose to go on a raid to the south of Noregr to the west. We all sang and told epic sagas of old warriors a lot like us that are now long gone, the sagas of Thor and his travels and other adventures and voyages we had been on in our young lives. The blood from my chest began to burst, the heat of the wine red blood burned me, keeping my conscious, it felt like my blood could flood the lands, that it can go on forever. I began to realise that I didn't know where I was going, I felt no hope or happiness in the direction I was going but I moved on, ignoring my body's warnings to stop. My wound had been done by a sword of a Saxon, the sword came across my right leg first then went for my torso, done like a dance it hit my chest and with ease, I swung my axe at his neck, he fell to the snow and I chopped his nape like a knife chopping vegetables. The cold began to embrace me, all feeling left, I fell to the white surface below but I did not care. I felt free and my eyes became dark and dimmer. The blood spilling around me creating a silhouette of my body. The last thing I see is the movement of a shadow, like the wings of a giant bird, I looked up as best I could and all I saw was a blinding light and a silhouette of a woman with wings, wearing a gorgeous armour, looking as if it had been crafted from the finest metals known to man. The very last thing I felt was the sense of leaving, but the feeling of forgetting something, leaving something behind. It was like I was above the clouds but dying in the snow. My eyes closed and I felt nothing.

POEMS

The Enchanted Encounter

"Who, oh who decorated the trees in the woods this
winter break?"
The locals asked as they peered through windows in
their wake.
"The tree ornaments are like no other we've seen
before,"
The children shouted as they ran excitedly out o'their
doors.
"Be gentle, they're not ours, we must take good care,"
The parents warned, "You mustn't touch, but you may
stare."

The marvellous occurrence of these little wooden tree
toys,
Became the talk of the town, the root of new joys.
The mystery was exciting, the spectacle now guarded,
A watchperson took shifts to protect these highly
regarded.
The details on the sweet little tree dolls, boasted much
care,
Much care from their creator, the details so rare.

The cloaks on the little wooden peg dolls were
stitched,
Embroidered beautifully, their decorations were
enriched.
Not a single soul would ever have been able to believe,

The enchantment the dolls would bless on those who did grieve.
When the stars shone and the winter moon glimmered late,
The dolls disappeared unnoticed by the guard who stood wait.

On they went drifting elegantly through the snowy forest,
On to the sleeping people unsuspecting of what was promised.
The dolls parted, assigned to individuals each, they arrived,
For one night only the people's loved ones were revived.
In the dreams of the bereaved, they were reunited one more time,
For one night only, this special blessing was simply sublime.

The night felt like an enchanted eternity for the chosen,
As they woke, their memories were cherished, frozen.
"Mummy, I dreamt of Grandpa last eve," one child said.
"Well so did I, how grand," revealed the mother, sat up in bed.
"I dreamt of my best mate," a neighbour later declared,
The theme became apparent as the news was shared.

"The tree ornaments have gone, they just
disappeared,"
The guard of last night anxiously declared.
"I don't understand how they could have vanished,
Not a soul passed me, I didn't leave my post, I'm
famished!"
"Ah, I wonder, perhaps it makes sense," another
pondered,
"Perhaps we were visited by the dolls, it was them who
wandered."

Stories and hypotheses circulated for a long while,
Although no-one knew for sure, the dreams made
them smile.
The tale was told each winter break, precious to this
place,
This place, which was visited one winter, by the dolls
with grace.
To this day not one person does know, where they
came from or went,
Like those who were dreamt of, neither forgotten for
the time they spent.

T.L. Williams

New Year's Day

On January the first, as I take down the tree,
I think on yuletides past, present, and what will be.
I look on to the year ahead, grateful for blessings endured,
With my family safe and happy, I smile, feeling assured.
The house to some seems empty, but I see it as fresh,
A blank canvas once more, for new memories to refresh.
We enjoy some home cooked grub, snacks and tv too,
Soon new plans and ideas occur; so much for us to do!

T.L. Williams

Shivering – A Villanelle

My shivery spine enshrines the cold
As icicles tumble from the eaves
And slippery paths threaten the old

Grasp on a stick to keep a hold
As sore feet crunch the icy leaves
My shivery spine enshrines the cold

A frozen lake makes people bold
As they tug at one another's sleeves
And slippery paths threaten the old.

A low sun on snow shines like gold
As light with shadow interweaves
My shivery spine enshrines the cold

Large snowballs are patted and rolled
And on the lake are glittering sheaves
But slippery paths threaten the old

Frost's delicate patterns on windows fold
telling stories to the one who believes.
My shivery spine enshrines the cold
And slippery paths threaten the old.

<u>Rosemary Phillips – January 2018</u>

Light in the Garden – A Sestina

Ghostly branches shiver in the moon light
as through a window the mind of a child
absorbs this scene composed by the frost
and watches the dawn break in a white world,
colourless, no grey roofs, no green grass,
then into this land of diamonds flies a bird.

The pale vista glows from the gold of the bird,
with its radiant colours in the first shafts of light.
But the water is ice with no grubs in the grass
and the hungry bird seems to look at the child
who gives a sad glance and sighs for the world
and for the life which dies because of the frost.

Sighs also for hearts that are hardened by frost.
Then the glow of the sun reflects on the bird
which shines as a beacon of hope in the world
and berries and nuts can be seen in the light,
as feeding begins with a smile from the child
and slowly cold white turns into green grass.

The garden delights in the green of the grass,
but one shady corner's still covered in frost
and sadness still tinges the joy of the child
who plays in the garden and talks to the bird
and the bird's pure notes unite with the light
as the sun for a moment warms up the world.

But cold hearts still spread chill in the world
and in the shady corner with colourless grass,
where brambles and briars keep out the light,
the green remains under a blanket of frost.
There no one can hear the song of the bird
but faintly there comes a sob from the child.

As on to the ground fall the tears of the child
which melt a small part of that frozen world.
Then softly come delicate notes from the bird
and the bird joins the child to sit on the grass,
on a small patch of green surrounded by frost
where together they sing encircled by light.

Cold light from the moon gives birth to the frost
and the tall blades of grass bow their heads to the child
as the bird's golden song resounds in the world.

Rosemary Phillips June 2015

Reframe January

Snowdrops.
Whispers of spring.
Early blossoms hang like candyfloss on dark branches.
Peace restored after the exuberance of yuletide.
Days stretch a little longer as light slowly returns.
Time to start afresh.
New year's resolutions not yet grown old.
For now anything still possible.
Another year come full circle.
The cycle begins again.

Nancy Cattini

Field-walking in December

We walked line abreast across the field,
heads down, staring at the ground,
searching for flints in the ploughed earth, with the
wind cutting through us like a knife. Eyes streaming,
noses running, hands frozen within gloves, we stooped
to pick up stones, looking for evidence of working, for
sharp edges, the mark of a human hand.

Each stone could be an arrow head, an axe, every
flake a clue to the past.
But soon every flint looked the same, frost shattered
or hand-worked, who could tell? Or care? Lost in the
misery of the cold we thought only of the pub and
hot coffee.

Caroline Morrell

Winter Thoughts

Fresh winds and the cold has arrived
We don jumpers and woolly socks
The trees shed their leaves in anticipation
Birds feed their young and nest early
Polar bears fatten up now to hibernate

Hoping that Covid has been cured forever
Deaths happened, less people roam the planet
Covid took them and so we mourn our folks
Vaccinations saved those strong enough
Others continue to fight the restrictions

National insurance goes up, jobs go down
People seek early fight for food and petrol
Mothers hold hands at food banks in hope
Those with money will delight in it now
There's enough food for all they say

Shops fill with Christmas lights and cards
Children gaze in awe at the wonderment
The fake reindeer pulls a sleigh all lit up
Christmas wreaths in the shops today
So, we hurry with Christmas lists in search

Dressed in dark colours, we snuggle up
The fires are lit the logs all chopped neatly
Christmas dinner tables laid; food cooked
Some will sleep on the streets again
Wakes, parties, weddings normality returns

We raise a glass to the future and say cheers
Grateful to be able to enjoy Christmas fun
Or maybe just grateful to have survived
Globally we all try to breath and move on.
To celebrate joys of Christmas this winter

Sue Hadley

Oblivion in Winter

A cold covid time came upon us
Throughout the world we perished
It's just a flu some said and moved on
People watched the races oblivious
In nightclubs they swarmed together

Then the ice gathered and we locked our doors
People sat out of the cold watching statistics
Charts of deaths as winter months ploughed on
We stood in the cold and clapped for NHS
Watching confused politicians run to our aid

A hard time we had of this pandemic
Hearts stopped breathing apparatus arrived
People didn't go out into this cold fearing
Turning on their heaters from the cold
Frost arrived as Christmas trees shivered

Baubles and cards put up in that winter
We attended funerals keeping safe distance
Then a vaccine saved us and we breathed again
We opened our curtains and walked freely
New hope now for snowy happy new 2022.

Sue Hadley

Snow Arrival

In that cold Shropshire winter
The snow did bring you home
Ice formed inside my windows
Lost, sad, spinning yet you were
Non directional and seeking

And the snow formed a bed
A cold white yet soft place
That we forbidden would lie
Frosty words exchanged again
Before our lives became entangled

The ice cleared your path
As my heart travelled with you
Then back to her you coldly fled
Did your longing and love last?
I longed for you to be mine

My mind now clear as I dressed
Gathering a spade I then swept
All remnants of the snow and you
Needing my own love to cherish
Welcoming a happy new beginning

<u>Sue Hadley</u>

In the Corner of My Eye This Winter

Today in the corner of my eye
I swear I saw you waiting
Forever watching in silence
I kissed your cushion again
It's a winter morning ritual for me
Asking if you slept well in heaven

Telling you the family's new stories
How we are all healthy and thriving
Your paperwork follows on after you
The wake, the gatherings, the chat
Lives moving on, winters arrival again
We held our breath a pandemic ensued

Then through the snow the angels came
Healing broken hearts in a cold lockdown
I will continue to watch for you
In the corner of my eye soulfully
Saying silent prayers for all who lost family.
Let winter flush all germs away to oblivion

We hope for a brighter new year.
Past present and future there for all
Hope for snow fights and snowmen
Baubles will sparkle carols all sung
Babies snuggled in Mother's arms
While watching in the corner of their eyes.

Sue Hadley

75

One Winter's Morn

Landscape vanished.
Smothered, buried
Calm and peaceful
Frozen flecks
falling from the sky
Silently cover the world below
All is veiled, pristine and white
Familiar places
Disappear from sight
Storm roared
Wind blew
Snow laden trees
Shimmer in the breeze
Iced windows
Filter the morning view
A world that's waiting
To start anew.

Lynda Jones
(Scribbling Scribes Creative Writing Group)

A Journey Home

Through dappled flakes of light in frosted woods
Where trees with leafy intent stand to the wind
And tiny budding blooms strain to gain the bright-
sunshine, that is the promise of spring
My feet crunch beneath me as a pheasant rises aloft
And a curious fox races across my path
The wind blows some leaves into a vortex
The echo of winter adorns the day

Although springs' pledge approaches
The stony cold sustains its grasp
And attempts to arrest the seasons change
Frozen pools retain their unyielding form
In shadows where the sun is masked
As the day's phase enters its final quarter
I hear the sounds of birds on high
And rustling in the thorny undergrowth

Day turns to dusk as my journey continues
And trades excitement for hunger
The track becomes my journeys' focus
Temperatures plunge, as does my resolve
Darkness pending, the day begins to fade
Limbs now weary, ask for rest
My mind is seeking out the peace
That only my memory can reveal

Pools of light spill onto the ground
From the windows I see

As an owl greets the night.
She is kneeling spellbound at the fire
Her eyes reflecting the suspense
Nursing a cup long gone cold
Her face, radiant from the warm glow
She looks up as I enter the door

I speak but my voice betrays me
I feel the warmth that is the woman I love
She sobs into my shoulder
And kisses my icy cold cheek
There is no speech, just an embrace
A hold that seems to last an age
Our mingled tears adorn her face
Rejoicing, I am home

George Bonner 2021
(Scribbling Scribes Creative Writing Group)

Haiku Poem

Red, yellow and brown,
Autumn's colorful landscape,
Falling all around.

Chill winds blowing in,
Bringing wild devastation,
Chaos abounds.

Ferocious, wild seas,
Bringing death and destruction,
Attacking our shores.

Drip, drip, flash of light,
Deafening boom overhead,
The deluge begins.

Sparkling white flakes fall,
Clean, white blanket coats our World,
Winter now is here.

Lynda Jones
(Scribbling Scribes Creative Writing Group)

WINTER ACROSTIC

W armed by the open fire, lights dimmed, music turned down lo **W**

I stare out into the cold comfortless darkness as I sip my Martin **I**

N earby an owl screeches and the fox skulks back into its de **N**.

T racks criss-cross the lamp lit street - a snowy muddle of paws and fee **T**.

E erie shadows silently shift with the wind, disturbing my peac **E**.

R eflecting on this wintry scene, I return to my fireside chai **R**.

Shirley Nelder
(Scribbling Scribes Creative Writing Group)

WINTER STORIES

The Ghost of Winter Present by T.L. Williams

It was the first time I'd been on the underground in November.
Not that there is anything special about November as opposed
to any other month when travelling on the tube. It was just that
because it was cold outside and the carriage I was in was
peculiarly empty, there was an eeriness in the air. I was on my
way home from a weekend of early yuletide shopping.
Exhausted. The swaying carriage hypnotically encouraged my
eyes to grow heavy like a restless infant in a rocking cradle. I
tried to fight it but must have succumbed to sleep as when I
woke an old weather-faced man was sitting in the seat opposite
to me. I smiled politely then removed my glance. I fleeted my
eyes back to his seat, he had vanished. My bewilderment jolted
my mind and my eyes shot open – I'd fallen asleep for much
longer than I'd originally suspected. The announcement on the
train's tannoy stirred me from my fuzziness:

THE NEXT STATION IS MARBLE ARCH. PLEASE
MIND THE GAP.

I gathered my bags and scurried off the train planting myself to
the back edge of the platform, leaning against the wall for
stability. I just needed a few moments to clear my head
following the lucid dream I'd just had but was soon on my way,
up into the open, albeit polluted, air of London again. The
bustling traffic of cabs and busses made me smile, for they were
so cliché of the city. The iconic red and black vehicles were
reflected in the toy models of tourist shops. They made me feel
as though I too could be one of the little figures I'd seen earlier
in a window display, lugging bags of shopping, watched by the
towers and architecture of the capital. With that thought I
shuffled to the coach stop and waited for my ride back home to
Oxford.
    I'd have happily given into sleep on the coach, but the image
of the earlier man distracted me from my exhaustion. I wasn't

entirely sure why for he was simply a figure in a fleeting dream. I'd never seen him before in my waking life, so why was his welfare bothering me so much.

When I arrived home I dropped my bags to the side of the hallway and sluggishly retreated to the sofa, paralysed for a time. The soles of my feet had disappeared it seemed, replaced with pain from badly fitting, albeit trendy, footwear. Once some feeling had returned to them, I pushed myself to get a drink and unpack whilst supper cooked.

"How was your trip?" a genuine welcome home from my housemate, Danny – but his voice startled me. "You look like you've seen a ghost!" he added appearing from his room.

I laughed under my breath, "I was just deep in thought. Great trip, thanks – I'm tried now though. How are things?" I enquired.

"All well, cheers. I gave the tree some thought," Danny revealed, a twinkle in his eye.

"Oh yeah," I waited amused, he must have been dying to share his musing with me. We both loved the season, neither of us religious, but nevertheless excited by the build-up, and magic that it brought.

"The thing is, as much as we both love the real ones, I fear that the kitten might hurt her paws on the needles..." he kept a straight face.

"The kitten?" I called as he retreated into his room, I waited at the door. Danny and I were good friends, both single from different circumstances, and neither of us interested in relationships now – more invested in life and what it had to offer. We'd known each other for years, originally introduced through a mutual friend. This year was our first in the new house which we'd saved up for and bought together. We provided each other companionship and stability, an arrangement which suited us both perfectly. Both of us were particular and houseproud, so there was never any frustration regarding the cleanliness or state of the place. Danny appeared again, his eyes sparkled, he wore a wide, closed-mouthed grin,

anticipating my reaction. In his gentle hold was a tiny Siamese
kitten meowing
affectionately.

"I don't understand, I thought we both decided that we
wouldn't have pets!" I put my arms out to take the adorable
feline. I hoped that Danny wasn't going to say that we were just
pet-sitting, because I'd fallen in love with its unusually large ears,
and sapphire eyes. As I stroked it, it purred rhythmically.

"We did, didn't we, but the thing is you know Heena's cat
had kittens a couple of months back?" he began, his
Liverpudlian accent stronger in this instance.

"Yeah..."

"Well, she had found a home for this one, an elderly man,
but she was too much for him and so she was given back to
Heena and Paul. They'd already decided to keep two of the
littluns, so they needed to give the third away. When I saw her
Facebook post I messaged and asked if we could have one as a
trial. I did some research; Siamese cats don't really malt, and we
can keep her as a housecat if you prefer? Perhaps I was too
hasty...I..."

"Danny..." I interrupted.

"Yes..."

"She's perfect!" I looked up from the kitten for a second to
smile at him, "Thank you."

Danny put his arm around me in a half hug, I leant my head
into his chest unable to return the gesture properly with my
preoccupied arms. His proximity excited the kitten who
charged up my shirt and leapt to Danny's chest then shoulder,
he a bit taller than me.

"We'll have to think of a name for her, I've been avoiding
calling her by any pet-names in case they stuck. Any thoughts?"
he fussed the kitten as she pressed herself into his neck.

"Hmm, well, how about you open this first?" I reached into
the inside pocket of my coat and took out a paper wallet.

"What's this?" Danny took it carefully, conscious of the
kitten balancing on his shoulder.

"Open it and find out – it's a belated housewarming present..." I teased.

Danny gasped as he saw the tickets inside, "You didn't?!"

"I did, West End, and front row too..."

"This will be crackin', *thank you!*" he beamed then as he thought it he said aloud, "How about a character name from the show, for the kitten?"

"Of course! What about Peggy?" I suggested.

"Yes! What do you think *Peggy*, do you like that?"

The kitten purred agreeably.

*

Peggy had settled in well; she'd taken to sleeping on my bed at night. Something both Danny and I would have regarded as improper just a week before, we were learning fast how we were powerless to resist anything she desired. With a heavy blanket over my duvet sprinkled with her warmth I was very content and had drifted off to sleep without much thought. I had dreamt for the past few nights but of nothing striking. Nothing like the sinister encounter that had shook me up on my recent commute. Honestly, I'd forgotten about it with the distraction of Peggy. Physically, safe and snug in my bed, my mind voyaged to my local city centre, of all places. It was one of those dreams where you are suddenly plunged into it consciously, but seemingly you'd already been existing in it for a while before. Nonsensical as dreams often are, the fleeting stranger appeared once more, this time from a beam of light. He was in a panicked state, surrounded by the sudden emerging elements; leaves rattled in the wind around us as we stood in the middle of the hectic road, somehow untouched by angry traffic. His scruffy hair was short and white, his dated clothes were torn and mottled. He took hold of my arms with his hands and asked me to help him, in a desperate rage, "You must help me, you simply must, please, I implore you...".

"What must I do?" I replied...

"You know..." he told me cryptically.

"But I don't...please...how?"

"You know," he repeated.

I could feel him slipping away, and immediately a whirlwind took him and he vanished into thin air. I was amidst a manic clutter of traffic, beeping their horns as they whizzed past either side of me. I frantically looked about, wondering how to make my way safely to the path. I woke up in a start, bolting upright in bed. My fright alarmed Peggy who shot off the bed and I presume into Danny's room as soon after he appeared at my door. I wasn't sure what to say for my mind was distracted by what felt like impressions on my forearm. I wanted to help the ghostly man, his grip on my skin still felt so real, it was as if he had been in my waking life, clasping onto me, like a vivid memory rather than a dream.

"Are you ok?" Danny asked.

"I think so – bad dream. Sorry, did I shout out?" I wondered.

"Nah, Peggy bolted into me room and pounced on me bed – I got up to investigate what had spooked her and noticed you sat up in a daze," he explained.

"Sorry Danny, I should let you get some sleep."

"Don't be silly, I'm up now, not just gonna leave you startled on your own. Tea or cocoa?" he asked.

"If you're sure, then, cocoa sounds nice, thanks – I'll be down in a moment."

Peggy followed him loyally down the stairs, nose in air and tail excitedly upright, hoping for some warmed 'kitten milk'. I reached for my dressing gown and fuzzy slippers and made my way to the kitchen.

The cocoa was both soothing and warming, Danny had topped it with cream and a sprinkling of cinnamon.

"Happy December, by the way," he said, joining me on the sofa. Peggy wandered into the room, licking her lips. She looked to me then Danny, trying to weigh up who was most likely to give her an extra treat, though of course neither of us would - she'd been spoilt enough, and we'd not risk *human* treats on her fragile tummy. She'd still try for the duration of our drinks only giving up when both empty mugs were on the coffee table. She then decided to snuggle between us, content by our blankety dressing gowns.

I looked at the clock, "So it is!"

"We've not really discussed *when* we'll put the tree up, it will be an adventure with Peggy, won't it! Perhaps we could go shopping for one tomorrow, or *today,* rather," I said.

"Sure thing, I've got no plans," Danny agreed. He waited a moment then said, "Did you want to talk about it..."

"Tree shopping?" I asked.

"Nah, your bad dream," he corrected.

"You'll think it stupid, I expect," I said.

"Why's that?" he rested his head on his hand which was propped up from his elbow on the back of the sofa.

"Well maybe you won't...I mean you don't believe in ghosts - nor do I, but then again we both agreed not to have pets and that changed - for the good of course!" I fussed Peggy affirming that I was not criticising our contradiction of having her.

"Well let's hear it then," he encouraged.

"It's probably *just* a dream...the thing is, they don't feel like *dreams*," I began incoherently.

"Perhaps you should start from the beginning," Danny helped.

"Yes, that would make sense, wouldn't it...when I was on the tube heading back yesterday I must have dropped off for a minute or so. I was in an empty carriage, but as I slipped in to sleep I dreamt that an old man was sat opposite to me. I hadn't seen him arrive and I was a bit taken by his appearance, he seemed *old fashioned...*"

"Like an elderly person might dress?" Danny enquired patiently.

"Yes, I suppose...but his clothes were also *tired.* When I tried to look back at him in my first dream he'd disappeared

and then I woke. It stayed with me, the weir͟
put it down to the randomness of it, but I t͟
that. It's difficult to explain, it was so vivid
rather than a dream." I looked to Danny
compassionately, not judging me for wha͟
overreaction over a sleepy hallucination.

"That was yesterday, so what happened tonight...did y͟
have the same dream?" he asked as he too fussed Peggy who
was purring affectionately.

"Not quite, this time I was in town, it was as if I was awake
again, then suddenly the same man startled me. He grabbed my
forearm and implored me to help him. He'd appeared in and
was taken by a sort of storm. If it was in a film I'd have thought
he'd come from another dimension. Then I woke up. The
thing is when I woke up this time I could still feel his grasp on
my arm as though he'd really had hold of me." I knew it
sounded silly.

"I've heard of vivid dreams, but not reoccurring ones, not for
real, anyway...perhaps in films or shows, like you say," Danny
stared into space in thought.

"It's bound to be something metaphoric, perhaps some
buried anxiety or the like," I surmised, brushing it off.

"Have you ever seen this man before, his face, specifically?"
Danny asked.

"No, not consciously, at least not as far I
remember...perhaps unknowingly in passing," I replied. I
glanced down to Peggy who was on her back, her paws folded
sweetly over her chest. Her head was upside down as she
looked out into the space of the room. I wondered whether the
room looked *upside-down* to her or whether her brain swapped
it around as she saw it. There was no sound in our still night-
time lounge and Danny and I were both deep in thought,
petting her soft, fine fur. It was her sudden scram that caused
our eyes to follow her path. She had darted out of the room
abruptly. As I looked from the floor, my heart jolted. The
apparition was in our room, standing still, staring intently at me.

89

ooked far less vivid and more ghostly than he had in my
eams. Danny, trying to understand my sudden plight, too
ooked in the direction of the intruder. Honestly it was a relief,
although alarming, to feel him jumping toward me...if he'd been
any closer to me we'd be a spitting image of Shaggy Rodgers
and Scooby Doo.

"You see it too?" I stated rather unnecessarily as Danny had
linked my arm and was staring wide-eyed at the thing.

"Is that him?" Danny replied, statuette of both movement
and his grip on me.

"That's him," I said.

We were both frozen, as the spectre lingered, his clothing
wasn't as clear as I'd seen it in my mind, for he was translucent
now, masking the details of himself. Thoughts wandered
through my head, do I address him, do we move, wait for him
to go?

Peggy returned, a sudden burst of bravery had overcome
her...she paced in slowly, her back arched, throwing little kitten
hisses between tiny growls at our unwelcome visitor. He didn't
look at her, his eyes remained fixed with mine. Unnervingly he
slowly raised a pointing finger, gradually fading away as Peggy
neared. When he'd completely gone Peggy slowly looked at us,
still hissing, and growling, as if to say, "*I didn't care for him.*"
We didn't either and was glad he had now left. Peggy stayed on
guard for another hour after the apparition had faded. She was
much calmer now but sweetly stayed at her station.

When the spectre had retreated Danny looked to me, pale
faced. A couple of strands of his hair had fallen over his
forehead, resting on his eyebrow, his eyes were still twinkling
but his face had dropped, and he still had hold of my arm, so
close to me that I could feel his heart racing in his chest. Every
time I thought he was going to speak, words failed to make it
out of his mouth, I wondered if he'd even been able to string
them together in his brain. I went first.

"I'm not sure if I'm glad you've seen it because it means I'm not seeing things or concerned; as you seeing it means it's probably real."

Danny slowly took his arm from mine, sitting up straighter than he had been when leant into me. He stayed close though, not shuffling away.

"I don't believe in ghosts," he said, finally.

"Nor do I, but I can't explain what we both just saw. Peggy saw it too, otherwise I'd presume we'd both talked each other into a shared delusion."

Neither of us said anything more, too bewildered to perhaps, or too tired. After a long while of *meaning* to get back to bed we must have unintentionally given into sleep, sitting awkwardly, propping one another up.

The sound of cars outside stirred me moments before Peggy's outstretched front paws did.

My movement in turn roused Danny, who looked momentarily confused, then startled on remembering the events of last night.

"How are you feeling?" I asked him.

"Muddled," he returned.

"You still up for tree shopping today? It might be nice to take our mind off of, well, yes," I said gently.

"Sure, I'm up for it, I'll put the kettle on eh?" Danny smiled. His eyes were bright as always, regardless of the exhaustion in the rest of his face.

Peggy greeted him keenly with a chorus of meows, once she worked out he was fidgeting towards the edge of the sofa ready to rise. I watched her as she tactfully walked with tail in the air, and her eyes on Danny, hardly looking where she was going.

I was slightly anxious to be left alone in the room, but it was daytime now and more than that, I was a grownup. Given, *grownups got scared sometimes* and I told myself that that was ok but being a grownup, I had the maturity to try to rationalise the situation. My first move was to open the curtains and let in the light, it seemed like a logical idea. Danny was back in a tick with a mug of coffee in his hand, the first of a few which I would stare into distractedly, today.

No sooner than I knew it, my nose was inhaling the warm, rich aroma of another cup as we sat in a garden centre café. Peggy had been content in her little kitten basket, fast asleep when we left.

"If we get the one we both like and leave the box out in a corner, Peggy might be satisfied with that," Danny suggested.

"Or she might hide in it - *once she's pulled the tree down*," I chuckled.

"Well unless we hang it from the ceiling, I guess it doesn't really matter which one we get," Danny reasoned lightly.

"Indeed. I like the idea of the box...we could decorate it somehow and cut little windows and paw holes in it," I sipped my beverage feeling cosy and relaxed.

"It's a plan then. Just the ornaments to choose and then we'll be on our way back home for Christmas." Danny warmed both his hands clasping them around his coffee cup.

I gazed around the café peacefully, taking in the sights of the centre as people carefully shopped for their Christmas displays. The sight of an old man sitting alone caused my heart to jump. Danny clocked my alarm, hesitantly following my gaze.

"It can't be," Danny said softly.

"It's his twin if not him," I stated.

Danny turned back to me, words hanging on the edge of his lips, he hesitated. His head bowed forward, closer to mine and he said in a low hum, "Do you think we should talk to him?"

My eyes trailed away in thought, *what would we say?* "Let's watch him for a bit, *inconspicuously.*"

Danny nodded, and though we were discreet in watching our doppelganger friend, we must have seemed like a couple who had just had an argument, sitting mutely, gazing occasionally at one another blankly. My mind was searching for anything to say in terms of small talk. Distracting thoughts raced past my mundane notions causing them to spin away distantly. Danny's expression mirrored my own, his mouth opening on occasion as he deliberated whether to say what he had articulated in his mind. His last attempt was cut by the voice of a café server who too was seemingly concerned.

"Excuse me sir, are you ok? Do you need assistance?" she asked the old man kindly.

From the corner of my eye, I watched as the elderly man stared at the lady, a picture of confusion painted on his face. He abruptly locked his gaze on hers, grasping at her arm, gaping straight up to her eerily, "I'm looking for my wife, *Peggy*."

Danny and my eyes shot centre gaging the other's reaction.

"*Peggy?!*" Danny mouthed to me.

I said nothing but carefully moved my gaze back to the conversation. My heart had stopped when the name has been dropped, not only that but the way he had took her arm, just as he – or his astral projection had done in my sleep. It was too much of a coincidence, surely. Seconds later I was met with an answer to that query.

"Hey, I know you, don't I? Have you seen my wife?" the man rose from his seat, shuffling over to me.

Before I could look to Danny, the waitress was addressing me, "Do you know this gentleman?"

"I, no, no I don't...he's familiar though," I admitted.

"Would you kindly sit with him, I'll get him a cup of tea," she replied.

"Here," Danny offered up a fiver to cover the cost, "keep the change, a tip."

The waitress smiled then disappeared behind the counter to organise the warm beverage. I looked to Danny, and then the old man. "Here, have my seat, I'll just get another chair for myself."

"Do I know you? Have you found my wife?" the man persisted.

"No sir, I don't think we have met before," I said, half believing it to be true.

"I know your face, I've seen you, you were going to help me. I've seen *him* too," the man pointed to Danny.

"What's your name mister?" Danny enquired.

"I, well..." he reached into his coat pocket, though still clearly desperate for someone to *help* him find his wife. His hand was shaky and his mind part vacant. He placed a collaboration of pocket possessions on the table, including a letter. It read;

Dear stranger,

If you are reading this, you may be in the presence of my elderly father, Mr Mickey Gambon. He is suffering from the early stages of dementia and has likely wandered away from home. He is missing my mother, Peggy, very much, she sadly passed away earlier this year. He is under twenty-four-seven care; however, he is a very crafty and intelligent man and has walked astray before.

If you have found this letter, and hopefully my father, please call me, Holly, on the number below.

Thank you.

I passed the letter to Danny, and looked to the elderly man, "Mr Gambon, I think I can help you."

"You can find Peggy?" he asked, a new focus was apparent in his eyes.

"I have a kitten called Peggy, would you like to come back to mine to meet her? I have your daughter's number; she will be able to talk to you about your wife. How does that sound, Mr Gambon?"

"I had a kitten, it was Siamese," he replied, finally engaged in a more-sensical conversation.

94

Danny looked to me, he too had realised that our kitten must have once belonged to Mr Gambon, *he* was the elderly man who had originally owned her.

"What a coincidence, come on then, it will be lovely for you to meet our little kitty," Danny said kindly.

As Mr Gambon stood up, the waitress, (who was moving swiftly, though carefully, with the professionally balanced teacup on tray), realised we were leaving.

"We've found a note, we'll get him back to his family, have the tea yourself love. Merry Christmas," Danny said in a hum to the waitress collecting up Mr Gambon's pocket ingredients from the table as I carefully guided him to the car park.

The drive home was quiet, I sat in the back with Mr Gambon. His hand was as cold as a corpse's, so I offered him my scarf, and he insisted on holding my hand all the way home. I didn't mind, if I could offer him some comfort and serenity from his troubled mind, it was the least I could do. Danny took care of bringing in the tree, (*which he has impulsively purchased as we were leaving the garden centre*), from the roof rack whilst I guided the poor confused gentleman inside our warm cosy home. As soon as Danny was through the front door we let Peggy in from the other room. By the sound of her unremitting meows, she seemed most offended by our absence, clearly not having slept through the entirety of our shopping trip.

"I'll put the kettle on for you Mr Gambon," Danny called through.

Peggy decided to inquisitively sway into the sitting room where I had invited Mr Gambon to sit. He was quiet now; oddly settled. I placed a blanket around his shoulders and was about to sit beside him when Peggy started to swear and hiss.

"Peggy, don't be so rude, this is Mr Gambon, he's our guest," I reassured her. Like many other pet owners, I spoke to her with the impossible assumption that she could comprehend my words. I picked her up, fussed her, and then settled her on Mr Gambon's lap.

"This is our Peggy, Mr Gambon. Is she much like your kitten?" I enquired.

"Identical. Hello my love," he replied.

I found his sudden tight-lipped manner somewhat alarming; it was as though he had suddenly experienced a personality shift. I wondered, perhaps it was a symptom of the dementia.

"Perhaps you'll let me take a photograph. Here, I have a polaroid, then you can take it home as a souvenir of your outing today." Mr Gambon didn't object so I picked up my camera and snapped a shot of he and Peggy. "As I'm sure you'll know, they take a moment to develop, some people say to shake them, some say not too. I'll leave it to your judgement. I just need to make a phone call Mr Gambon; you stay here with Peggy. Danny will be in soon with a nice cup of tea." Once I'd placed the photograph on his knee, I hovered a moment. Peggy was licking her paws on his lap as he silently stared eerily into space.

Danny stood over three mugs, tactfully taking the tea bags out of each before adding a drop of milk.

"I'm going to make the phone call," I told him, "do you have the note?"

"How is he?" Danny wondered, talking quietly under his breath so not to be overheard by our guest. He passed me Holly's letter.

"Very quiet," I replied before tapping the number into my phone. Danny stood with back to counter, hovering whilst I made the call.

"Hello? Holly? ...Hi, hi! Holly, I found your number on a note.....I'm sorry – could you say that again please, the line went a bit funny...Last week you say? I, oh my, I...I'm so very sorry to hear that... Next week? I see, gosh... Well, thank you, we'll see what we can do. Where will it be held?... Ok sure, well we'll try our best. Listen, I'm very sorry again, if we don't meet you next week then here's wishing you a very peaceful Christmas. Take care won't you... Ok, thank you, goodbye, bye now."

My hand shook as I took my phone from my ear to end the call.

Danny's expression was one that I had seen a fair few times recently.

"Danny, will you go and give that tea to Mr Gambon please?" I asked, trying to compose myself.

"Am I going to find Mr Gambon in the front room if I do?" he replied.

"Honestly, I hope not."

We exchanged a look of horror. Words did not need to be spoken to negotiate the need for one another's company. Together we slowly walked into the front room, Danny had sensibly left the tea on the side. Once we dared to look to the sofa it was clear that what we had both feared and hoped was true; Mr Gambon was nowhere to be seen. The blanket was draped on the back of the sofa, Peggy had not moved – still contentedly licking her paws. Next to her was the polaroid photograph. I was almost too afraid to pick it up, I couldn't not look, however. Slowly, somehow terrified that the old man would rematerialize, I leaned forward, pinching the polaroid snap from where it sat. The photo had taken, but it had not taken the image I saw through the lens of the camera, instead simply the scene that sat before us now.

I turned to Danny, "I took this photo of Mr Gambon, just two minutes ago."

"What did Holly say on the phone?" Danny asked.

I turned to look at his sparkling eyes, the brightness of which gave me the courage to relay what I had been told on the phone. "Mr Gambon, Holly's father, died peacefully in his sleep at home last week. He apparently had lost this note the last time they had taken him to the garden centre. His funeral is next week, she invited us to attend. I thought perhaps we could send flowers?"

"I think that would be nice. I don't understand it though. The waitress at the café saw him too, you held his hand, gave him your scarf...where is your scarf?"

"He couldn't have wandered off could he? Perhaps he was someone else's father? He could have picked up the note...." I tried to comprehend.

"I set the alarm on the door...if he'd have walked out we'd have known...and you know how skittish Peggy is, she'd have jumped off if he'd have gotten up," Danny reasoned.

We searched the house anyway, even opened the door – of which the alarm did sound, causing Peggy to tear out of the sitting room and up Danny's leg and back to his shoulder. Mr Gambon was nowhere to be found.

We sent flowers and a card to the funeral. I popped our return address on the package in case they didn't make it safely in time. A Christmas card through the door the following week informed us that they had and were '*warmly* appreciated'. It was from Holly, she had thanked us for the flowers and for our concern. She also noted that she was moved to see that we were the buyers of her parents' home, '*an incredible coincidence*', she said. If only she had known that we were also the owners of her father's rehomed kitten. There had been no sightings of Mr Gambon, or my scarf since, nor could we work out how his spirit, or whichever part of him it was that we had *met,* had found us. Nevertheless, it was enough to believe he was now at peace.

It was nearly Christmas. Finally, the tree was decorated, as was Peggy's 'Christmas den' – which she *loved!*

"These gingerbread men are delicious Danny," I complimented, dipping one into the squirty cream atop my hot chocolate. Christmas music played joyfully in the background...a track just finishing blended into 'Slade's '*Merry Xmas Everybody*'.

"I love this song," Danny said, "Let's dance!"

"You are spoiling me today, buddy!" I replied, carefully placing my Christmas treats on the coffee table.

Danny moved it aside, then took my hand as we swayed, twirled, and jumped around to the rocky Christmas hit. With wide eyes, Peggy bobbed her head watching us with fascination. It was the start to the remainder of a very merry Christmas indeed.

The doorbell rang, abruptly interrupting our jovialities.

"Who would that be on Christmas day?" I wondered aloud.

"I'll see to it, here dance with Peggy for a mo," Danny said scooping her up gently into my arms. Seconds later he returned.

"Who was it?" I asked.

"There was no-one there, just this package, the label says it's fer you." Danny passed it to me, taking Peggy.

I opened the package carefully, wondering who it was from, and why it had been left for me. Though not for long. From beneath the safety of the wrapping, I pulled out a familiar item. My missing scarf.

A wintry extract of online novel, '*Drowned Hogg Day*' - by Nick Smith

Alex Hogg's blog, Wednesday 28 December 2016

Oxfordshire village, Wham! yet empty inside (6)

A few days after Christmas in 1810, Thomas Jefferson Hogg had Univ almost to himself. He and Shelley (who was still partying at Field Place) exchanged daily letters but Hogg could not bear to sit shivering in his rooms waiting for his chum to return for Hilary Term. So Tom All-Alone equipped himself with strong shooting-shoes and gaiters, as well as copies of Virgil's *Georgics* and *Aeneid*, and walked out into the icy wastes of South Oxfordshire on a solitary pilgrimage to the cathedrals of Winchester and Salisbury, then (like Tess) to Stonehenge itself. After several days combating hypothermia and truculent yokels, he trudged back to college again with enough anecdotes to fill up a self-indulgent chapter of his ill-fated *Life of Shelley*.

I too long to escape from my solitary abode and lose myself in the eerie calm of the wintry landscape. Different shrines tempt me. I could drive down to Sparsholt and walk the Ridgeway to Goring to pay my respects at the house where George Michael died alone three days ago. I might even walk another few miles further east to Friar Park, last home of another saintly George, humming 'While My Guitar Gently Weeps' as I go. Georgics, indeed.

But the fog is so thick this morning that there has been a 20-car pile-up on the A40. I leave the Yaris slumbering under its frosty winter coat and embark on a more modest walking-tour. I head up the Thames towpath to Jericho where St Barnabas Church towers forbiddingly over terraced streets built for iron-workers and bookbinders. It is impossible to guess which bits of masonry a young Thomas Hardy would have worked on.

From there I cross a shimmering Port Meadow towards the *Perch* and head north to Godstow, then under the ring-road to Wytham, pausing for a light and lonely lunch at the *White Hart*. The frosty antennae of beeches and sycamore beckon me further but I do not know the way through the woods and I turn back towards Wolvercote and the metropolis beyond. I pass the bridge club south of Summertown and head for the Parks, hoping to check out the location of the Clones' pipe-dream next July. But, like Sir Gawain on his post-Christmas trek or Aeneas as he avoids drowning in the whirlpool of Charybdis, I have only the haziest idea where to go.

That gig is the one thing I have to live for, I decide, the one reason for hoping that Solomon Sage had it wrong all along. I try again to think of what dying would be like, but draw a blank – it is so hard to contemplate nothingness in the midst of life.

I have no job, no home, no one to love. Yet, despite everything, I do not want to die. As I complete my uneventful round trip, I catch myself praying for time.

*

You can find the online novel at the following web address:
https://drownedhoggday.wordpress.com/2016/12/29/wednesday-28th-december

A walk down Memory Lane at Christmas by Sandra Pickworth

Ellen sat in her chair next to the fire and took a sip of Mulled wine.

Today was Christmas Eve. It had been a long day doing housework, making mince pies and icing the Christmas cake.

Tomorrow the family would be arriving mid-morning to spend Christmas together.

Ellen left the Christmas cake decorations for William, age 7 and Charlotte, age 5 to decorate the cake. It was a family tradition for the children to decorate the Christmas cake.

Eddie was sitting in his chair doing a crossword puzzle. He said he was stuck on one clue – "'Duel with Yeti.'"

Ellen picked up the Radio Times to see what was on television on Christmas Day. The Queen's speech at 3pm, Strictly Come Dancing and Call the Midwife in the evening. Ellen set the programmes in to record because the family liked to play board games and charades after lunch on Christmas Day.

Ellen's mind drifted back to her childhood in the 1960's and some of the programmes on television on Christmas Day. Ed 'Stewpot' Stewart did a programme from a hospital children's ward in the morning. In the afternoon Billy Smart's Circus followed by a pantomime in the afternoon. At some time over Christmas, Top of the Pops was on too. It was fun waiting to find out which song was the Christmas number one.

Christmas Day started early, waking up to see if Father Christmas had been. Some presents Ellen remembered receiving were Painting by Numbers from Auntie Mary and

103

Uncle Stephen, A book of Fairy Tales from Uncle Jo and her best present of all, a teddy bear from Mum and Dad.

Ellen came back to the present and looked across at Eddie, engrossed in the crossword puzzle. She said, "Do you remember when we were teenagers and the Christmas disco at youth club and carol singing on Christmas Eve?"

Eddie smiled remembering. "Yes," he said. We and a group of friends went carol singing with the curate and choir master. We always ended up at the club near church. After we had sang to the adults who had been dancing the evening away in the large hall, we were invited to help ourselves to what was left of the buffet in the snooker room."

"Yes," said Ellen, "then some of us went to church for the midnight service. You and I and other bell ringers rang the church bells."

Eddie laughed and said, "I expect the neighbours thought, 'Hark those bells do ring.'" Ellen laughed too.

Back to the present and Ellen made supper for her and Eddie. Then at 11.15 pm she said, "Come on Eddie, it is time to go and ring the bells for the midnight service. Oh, and the answer to the crossword clue is, Yuletide."

A Child of the Solstice by Hugh Westbrook

For as long as William could remember, the Winter Solstice was the most exciting time of the year. Not for him though. No, his parents seemed to be the ones experiencing an almost overwhelming delirium the closer the day came. William could never comprehend their increasing anticipation as the day grew closer. To him, it was just a cold, dark day. But to his parents, it was the greatest twenty-four hours of the year.

As he grew up, the routine became the same. Before the day had even dawned his parents would bid him farewell, leaving him in the capable hands of his aged aunt and uncle, Ivy and Jack, who remained sprightly despite their advanced years and Jack's pronounced limp. They walked him to school, played with him when he was at home and cooked up a superb dinner which was ready just as his parents returned from wherever they had been, bright-eyed and exuberant. They would exchange a knowing look with Ivy and Jack and that would be the end of it. He never knew where they went.

When he was very young, he imagined they were off on all kinds of adventures, meeting dragons or knights or aliens, but as his teenage years kicked in and his hormones engaged, his thoughts became more coarse as he figured they just needed some time to themselves to do what loving adults do together. It now seemed more inappropriate that they shared that look with their ancient relatives when they got back. But if Ivy and Jack were winking at them he would never know – their glasses were so thick that their eyes remained an almost cloudy blur behind the extravagant lenses.

It all changed once he turned eighteen. A week or so before the Solstice, William's parents sat him down at the kitchen table. They had a serious look on their faces and William was worried. The cottage felt cold. There was no noise apart from the large wall clock pronouncing the passing of seconds. The Cotswold stone walls never really cheered him and the expanses of forest and field outside always made him slightly nervous. The forbidding expressions his parents were wearing only added to his nerves.

"What is it?" he blurted out.

His father stared at him once more, and then his face burst into a huge smile. Now William didn't know what to do.

"Your mother and I agree," he said. "It's time."

"Time for what?"

"You're of age now. It's time to make you part of our Solstice celebrations."

Given what his teenage mind had concluded that their celebrations consisted of, this pronouncement worried William even more. He gulped and left his thoughts unspoken. There would be time later to object.

There was a knock at the door. William's mother smiled and got up to answer it. When she returned a few minutes later, Ivy and Jack were with her. And she was carrying a large, and very old book. She put it down on the table.

William quickly reasoned that this wasn't an antique volume of the Kama Sutra. So what to make of it?

"This," said his mother, reverently patting the soft brown leather of the volume in front of her, "This book. This is our book of Solstice magic."

Momentarily, William wished that his initial suppositions had been correct. At least he might have been able to make some sense of that. But this?

"The Winter Solstice is a time of magic," his mother explained gently. "And we have become rather good at magic."

"Pulling rabbits out of hats at children's parties?" William inquired, more in hope than anything else.

"No," his father smiled back and fixed him with a dazzling green stare. "Not party tricks. Real magic. And we have had some help," and he looked at Ivy and Jack. William was now even more bewildered.

"Let me explain," Jack said kindly, and he told William about a time of a quarter of a century before, when he had started teaching William's father the rudiments of ancient magic and had invited him to attend classes with him and Ivy. It wasn't long before Ivy met his mother at the local library and brought her along too. "And as the magic blossomed in their hands, so it did in their hearts as well," Jack finished.

William's parents gave him a look that suggested that was laid on a little too thick, but Jack kept his counsel behind his thick glasses.

They quickly explained the rest. They had found themselves drawn to the Winter Solstice, with its traditions of feasting and revelry and its rituals spanning time and space, from Ancient Greece and Rome through Asia and South America, as well as back in England. And as they studied the traditional magic of their homeland, so they found they were able to perform some of their own.

Time became their obsession. After all, the Solstice was associated with time, the shortening of the days and the promise of longer ones to come, so time magic felt like the right thing to do. But nothing they tried quite worked – stopping time, making time go backwords, slowing time down or speeding it up. Nothing quite succeeded.

"But then we cracked it," his father said.

"What do you mean cracked it?" William asked. What on earth had they done.

His father beamed with the excitement of a precocious child about to tell

his parents that he had come top in a big test at school. "We invented the Time Door."

"What's the Time Door?"

"I'm glad you asked. We could tell you. But we'd rather show you."

And so it was that William found himself in some remote countryside a distance from home, at an hour so ungodly that even the birds had not yet stirred to begin their morning chirruping. He and his parents stumbled through tree roots and bracken, with their torches lighting their way through the enveloping blackness, though they did little to stave off the freeze of the winter morning, and William was convinced that his breath would escape him as an ice block rather than just a fine mist.

Eventually they stopped fighting their way through foliage and came to a hill. They climbed for a few minutes, surrounded by dips and crevices, before stopping near what appeared to be a large grey mark, around ten feet high. "And now we wait," William's father said.

"For Godot?" William asked.

"Very droll. No, now we wait for the Sun."

William scratched his head. Were his parents now Sun worshippers?

"We'll have a drink while we're waiting," his mother said, and his parents put down the vast rucksacks they were carrying.

"What have you got in there?" William asked, as his mother pulled out a flask and started pouring tea.

"Just everything we need. Food, drink, first aid kit, guns, hand grenades, some larger explosives, flame throwers. Just the basics."

"Very funny. Payback for my Godot joke."

"No, that was just a poor joke. What I said is true," and William's father proceeded to show his slack-jawed son the full armoury that they were transporting. "Drink your tea," he advised with a smirk. "It's almost time."

William sipped his drink and tried to grasp what was going on around him. But he couldn't really. "So how long do we sit here?" he asked eventually.

"The sun comes up a few minutes after eight. We start our magic a few minutes before that, so pretty soon. Then you'll see something."

William sat silently in the dark, trying to stay warm, as the clock ticked on slowly. As it finally dawdled its way to eight o'clock, his parents stood up, pulled some random wooden objects out of their voluminous bags and placed them in front of the large grey mark, before they began chanting in a language at whose origin William could not even begin to guess. He wanted to ask them what was going on but thought it better not to interrupt their flow. Hopefully this would all be over in a few minutes and he could go home and have a bacon sandwich. There's probably one in those bags, he thought to himself, along with a nuclear bomb and a Kalashnikov.

The chanting got louder, reached a peak, and then stopped as his parents stood back to either side of the grey mark. Second later, the first inklings of the sun peeked over the horizon, and speckles of sunlight hit the area. William looked intently at it, the first light of the day was definitely a thing of beauty. And it seemed strangely alive, dancing on the surface in front of him, changing colour, yellows and blues, greens and reds, it was transfixing.

And then the whole surface flashed a brilliant orange and started shimmering and shaking in front of him. He stood up and backed away. What was happening?

"Welcome to the Time Door!" his father said.

"What? What is it?"

"It is a door to another time on the day of the solstice, and it will stay open until the sun sets in around eight hours. And we can go through it to see what's on the other side."

111

"I'm sorry."

"It's a gateway to a different time."

"Oh Time Travel. Well that's all right then. I thought you were going to tell me something nuts. Time Travel! That's fine then, totally normal. Can we go home now?"

"No. You're coming with us. And you'll find this is true."

William looked to his mother, then his father, then his mother once more, but he could see that they didn't appear to be joking. Maybe he would have to play along for a few minutes, show willing and indulge his parents to get through this. Maybe he would have to walk forward into the orange light and bang his nose against the surface behind it before this farce would be over. Maybe him sustaining a black eye would be enough to placate them.

And so he strode forward purposefully straight into the light.

But the clunk he expected never came.

A few seconds later he found himself back where he had started. Only now there was thick snow on the ground. And some trees he didn't recall having seen in the moments before. And a grey and cloudy sky, rather than the clear pale blue one which had recently been appearing. And his parents right behind him, grinning in triumph at what they had just achieved.

"What? Where?" William stammered.

"Come with us," his father said, and his parents set off towards the top of the hill, with William stumbling in pursuit as he tried to adjust to the piles of snow now covering his boots, the flakes wafting into his eyes and the general absurdity of the situation.

As they reached the top, William began to recognise the spot. "I've been here," he said. "Oxford's in the distance."

"That's right," said his mother. "That's why we start here. It helps us to tell when we are."

"When we are?"

"Yes, when we are. The Time Door takes us to another time for a few hours, but we don't control it and we don't know where in time we have travelled to. So we have to work it out. That's part of the fun."

William rubbed his eyes. He still struggled to believe that this was possible. But he also couldn't deny that the weather and the landscape were the same and yet vividly different from what he had been experiencing just a few minutes before.

"Here we are." William's father reached into his bag and took out a very sophisticated looking pair of binoculars, before training them in the direction of where Oxford was. Or rather, where the Oxford that William knew should have been.

After a few minutes, he passed the binoculars to William and he peered through them. "It looks different," he gasped.

"It is," his father said euphorically. "It definitely is."

William took the binoculars and trained them on Oxford. But where he should have seen the gleaming spires and domes of the famous city, he instead saw a smaller space and thick city walls. "I don't understand."

"I think we're in medieval times. I can't be sure exactly, but maybe nine hundred, a thousand years before our time. That's the Oxford you are looking at," and he passed the binoculars to William's mother, who studied the scene for a minute or so and then nodded her assent.

"So now what?"

"Now we explore."

"All the way over there."

His father chuckled. "No, we never go to Oxford itself, it's a long way and it's not sensible to venture there. But we can look around here and see what's what."

As they trudged down the hill, William's parents explained a bit more about their solstice ritual. Every year, the Time Door took them to a different, random point in time, and they then spent the daylight hours exploring, always making sure to get back to the door before the last sunlight disappeared.

The time was random, and as far as they could tell, never repeated itself, making the anticipation of when they might end up all the more energising. They took care on their travels, avoided contact as much as possible, watching from afar when they could, travelling with a battery of weaponry and other 21st century tools which meant that they always felt they moved around in relative safety.

"But what if you end up in the future?" William asked.

"It hasn't happened yet," his father replied. "But if it did, I suspect we may not stay that long. We prefer not to take risks."

William's scepticism had vanished, to be replaced by the wonder of where he now found himself. He was in twelfth-century Oxfordshire with his parents, seeing sights that nobody else in his lifetime had seen. He could feel that the countryside seemed different, wooded areas were thicker, hedges seemed more random, the air seemed brighter, the snow seemed cleaner. Everything felt the same, and then different.

Many things were familiar over the next few hours. The handful of birds in the sky, the colour of the clouds, these felt normal to him. But the people that he saw were very different. They were dressed in greys and browns, they seemed smaller somehow, stooping more, as they worked through their days, fetching and carrying. This was all seen from a distance, his parents advised that they should avoid being seen or interacting with people as much as they could, so they stood behind trees at the edge of villages and saw the people milling around, though truth be told there were few of them because of the strength of the snow, and instead William found himself looking at the wooden buildings, structures he had only seen in recreations now laid bare in front of him as real life, with a slightly acrid smoke invading his nostrils throughout as the villagers burned what they could in an attempt to stay warm.

What he hadn't been prepared for was the noise, or rather the lack of it. Modern life is full of sound, from traffic and aeroplanes to the general hubbub of the greatly increased population to the indeterminate hums of electricity pylons or mobile phone towers. But this landscape was bereft of all external noise apart from occasional birds or insects, or random clinks from the village suggesting labourers at work, and with the snow acting as an added soundproofing device, the silence was almost deafening.

The hours flew by. William could scarcely believe it when after looking in on three or four villages, his parents said it was time to head back to the hill. Given the weather in particular, they wanted to give themselves plenty of time. "We want to be here, but we don't want to stay here," his father cautioned.

And so they found themselves back in front of the shimmering orange light as the sun began to descend, and with one final look around, they stepped back through to their own time, with the ground clear once more and the sound of activity now prevalent in the distance.

William could now understand why his parents seemed to work themselves up into a frenzy the closer the Solstice came. They had told him he could speak to nobody about it apart from themselves, Ivy, and Jack, but he couldn't stop thinking about the experience and willing himself towards it again. The long summer days seemed to ramble on forever, while his parents disappointed him by saying they couldn't extend the magic into the summer solstice as well. The coming of autumn was no longer a disappointment at the decline of the fine weather, it simply meant the onset of winter and one day closer to another trip. And as December started, it was all he could do to stop telling everyone he spoke to that he was close to another epic adventure.

The second visit through the Time Door was very different. The weather felt much warmer than the frosty morning they had left behind as soon as they stepped through, William quickly found himself taking his hooded coat off due to a few prickles of sweat. The sense of being somewhere else only intensified as they reached the top of the hill and looked towards Oxford with the binoculars. There was no Oxford to be seen.

"We're pre-history," his father said with excitement. "The landscape will look different in many ways. But it also means we need to be even more careful. There are no domesticated animals here, no experience of humans at all. We need to be on our toes."

And so it proved. While the untamed countryside, with its many unfamiliar trees and plants, proved endlessly diverting, the constant movement and rustle from animals who were not commonly found roaming around near modern-day Oxford meant they were always on alert. It was fine when they were at a distance watching elk and deer grazing in the vast swatches of unruly grass, or even when they could see wolves or bears running far away, but whenever they heard scampering or snuffling near them, they had to remain vigilant. The constant worry gnawed away at them and detracted from the brilliance of what they were seeing, with the greens and browns of nature seeming more vivid than they ever had before.

As the afternoon wore on and they thought about heading back, they heard a few bumps and bashes in the trees surrounding them. They turned to see a wild boar hurtling straight towards them. The beast fixed them with an angry glare as it hurtled in their direction, but William's father nonchalantly pulled out a gun and fired, hitting it between its irate eyes and sending it crashing to the ground. The sound of the bullet seemed to echo for an eternity, such was the silence which it punctured.

"Wow," William said.

"Always got to be on your toes," his father replied. "I don't think we have altered history unduly there. Well, except for that poor creature, I suppose."

The next 12 months passed much as the previous ones had done. The Time Door was now like a drug for William, he couldn't go for a day without thinking about it, speculating on where they might end up next, reading endlessly about the eras they had visited so far, nagging his parents about finding ways to utilise it more often. Jack and Ivy just smiled indulgently as they watched him prod at them for the umpteenth time.

The third trip was the most modern so far. Oxford looked much more like the city they knew, and their observations and discovery of a discarded newspaper near a local village confirmed they had only gone back around 150 years. "Victorian Britain," his mother mused, and they all noted how the countryside was feeling much more familiar, the buildings more modern, the noise more familiar.

But the dangers also felt different. There were more people around than William had been used to on previous visits, people in carriages and horses seemed to be constantly in their eyeline, despite the uneven and cold ground and the persistent drizzle which danced down their faces. Staying out of sight was proving harder than before. William loved this, but it also came with stresses, and sometimes the greatest moment of the whole journey came from the exhilaration of their safe return and the memories they would hold on to forever.

They had about an hour before sunset and had started their way back through the woods when they became aware of people nearby. The movement was erratic, it seemed to coincide with their own steps. "I think someone's following us," William's father muttered.

"What do we do?" his wife asked.

"We stay calm. Here," and he handed the others a pistol each. William felt panic rising. The only weapon he had ever held had fired imaginary bullets at a TV screen.

They went a little further forward. There was tell tale crunching once more. They paused. They looked around.

"Let's just go and not stop," William's father said. "We can defend ourselves against whatever they've got."

The three of them bowled forward, starting to break into a run as they dodged the trees. Now they could hear footsteps behind them, three, maybe four sets, pounding the same ground as them, getting a little closer.

"We've got to get away," William's mother panted.

"Stop!" yelled a voice from behind them.

They ignored it and kept going.

"Stop or we'll shoot."

They ignored it and kept going.

Three shots rang out.

William's father fell to the ground.

"Dad!"

"It's OK, it's my leg." He tried to stand up again. He fell down again.

"Get rid of them. Somehow!" he tried to shout, weakly though.

The footsteps were much closer now. William could see them. Four bearded men, carrying rifles, who didn't look much like they wanted a convivial chat about the scenery. He was rooted to the spot. He had no idea what to do.

Out of the corner of his eye, he saw his mother throw something and a few second later, there was an explosion in front of the men. One of them fell, the others whirled round in confusion. Another throw. Another explosion. The men tottered backwards. A third. The men scattered. The danger was over.

Except that it wasn't. William's father looked pale, there was sweat on his face. His leg was bleeding profusely. William's mother quicky pulled out the first aid kit and started putting pressure on it, looking for bandages, anything to stem the bleeding and halt the pain.

"What are we going to do?" William spluttered.

"We? We aren't going to do anything. Me? I'm going to stay here and get your father better. You are going to go home."

"No!"

"Yes! Listen to me. Listen to me!" William's mother grabbed him by the arms and held him rigid. "Your father and I agreed. We would never put you in danger. If anything should ever happen to either one of us, we had to make sure that you got back safely."

"I didn't agree."

"You didn't get a vote. You have no choice. You have your whole life ahead of you, you're not going to miss it because of what we've done."

"But I can live it here with you."

"No. No, you can't. You have to go back."

"I won't leave you."

"You must."

William's mother turned back to his father and applied further pressure to his leg. It seemed to be stemming the bleeding.

"Come on, he can walk with us."

"I can't son. I can't," his father replied

"No!" William wailed

"You must go," his mother said. "You must go now. Before it's too late."

William stared at his parents through his sodden eyes. He couldn't believe he had to leave them here. In the past. He couldn't believe he'd never see them again. "I'll come back. I'll find you," he sobbed.

"I know you'll try. I love you so much," his mother said.

"I love you too," his father added through the pain. "Now go!"

William gave them a final look and then turned and ran, knowing that had he hesitated a moment longer, then he would have hesitated forever. He ran and ran up the hill until he found the Time Door, and without another look he bolted straight through it before collapsing back on the other side, back in his own time, bereft of his parents, crying like he was back in their arms as a newborn, inconsolable.

He stumbled slowly down the hill to where they had left the car. He had a key, he was grateful at least for that, but he didn't know how he drove it home. It was all a blur to him. His driving sense took over and got him home safely.

He walked in and saw Jack and Ivy sitting there, staring intently at him through their thick spectacles. He flung himself into a chair without even taking his coat or boots off and howled with anguish.

His aged relatives went over to him and sat on either side of him. "What's wrong dear?" Ivy asked.

"They've gone. They've gone."

"Who's gone?"

"Mum and Dad. Dad got injured. I had to leave them. They're gone. They're trapped. 150 years ago. I have to go back. I have to find them."

"You know you can't. You know that's not how it works."

"I'll find a way. I'll make it better. They found a way. I just need to find a better way."

"Or maybe you don't."

William looked up. "What do you mean?"

Jack looked serenely at William and took off his glasses, fixing him with a kind stare. A piercing green stare.

"Dad?" William gasped.

Jack patted him on the hand.

Ivy took off her glasses.

"Mum?" William gasped again. "But how?"

"Well dear," his mother replied. "When we'd found a way to get your Dad better again, established ourselves as travellers and found a place to live, we set about solving some of the other mysteries of time. Seems like we found a way to make time slow down after all. For us at least."

"So, so, I don't understand."

"We were determined we'd see you again. So we sold some of what we had brought with us to collectors of curios, that set us up for some time, and used all our other knowledge to make lots more money. And we devoted ourselves to slowing our lives down, so we could see you again. And we have certainly done that. We got to watch you grow up twice."

"So you're not my uncle and aunt."

"Never were," his father twinkled. "As we got older and became more accustomed to our older faces, we realised who Jack and Ivy really were. And we remembered how they had come into our lives, so we just followed the script we had already seen. I pretended to be a distant great uncle who nobody really remembered. And I knew that nobody ever checked these things out, so they just accepted me."

"And I befriended your mother, sorry young me, through book clubs and the library," his mother added. "And so we taught them both."

"And you didn't tell them, sorry you, sorry them, who you were?"

"No."

William was having trouble getting his head around all of this. But he had experienced the same issue when first confronted with time travel, and he had come to terms with that. So why not this. Especially as he had his parents back.

"But why teach them?" he blurted out. "Why let them, you, go through the Time Door at all, if you knew that one day, you'd never come back?"

"Because we had to."

"Why?"

"Because if we hadn't gone back then we couldn't have taught ourselves the magic."

"But that's just daft You're saying you needed to go back so you could get trapped and then live a long life and then teach yourselves the magic just so you could go back and get trapped. It's self-fulfilling. If you hadn't taught yourselves the magic you wouldn't have needed to learn in the first place. It doesn't make any sense."

"Yes it does," his mother said gently. "Because that wasn't the only thing we did."

William paused. And blanked. And then he realised.

"Because you made sure you met each other. Wow."

"So we had to get stuck. If we hadn't been stranded, we never would have met in the first place. So even though we knew how it would play out, we couldn't stop it."

"Even though you knew you'd leave me without you."

"But we haven't. We knew we'd still be here when you got back. Just a little bit older."

William shook his head again. This was far too much to deal with. But he would manage to. After all, they were a family again.

"And think about this," his father added. "If we hadn't made sure that we'd met, there would be no you."

William drew a sharp intake of breath. "That's a thought."

His parents smiled at him. "Yes it is. You really are a true child of the solstice."

Proof by Melissa Westbrook

This time there were two.

They arrived outside breathing clouds of icy fire, insipid light dimly illuminating the precarious heap of technical sundries that threatened to swallow them whole.

"Careful! Those full-spectrum cameras are expensive" snarled the tall one, oblivious to the smirk and exaggerated eye-roll he received from beneath layers of gawdy, multi-coloured fleece.

The heavy wooden door uttered a guttural moan as it was forced out of its slumber. Even I had to admit that it was all a bit of a cliché and yet the two approached with reverence, eyes awash with a heady mixture of hope and fear. I watched them point out the darkest, dampest corners transforming intricate cobwebs into a tangled nest of wires. The tall one stumbled close to me making me flinch. I was being irrational, of course, as I am long gone.

Then I watched them
wait
and wait
and wait
and wriggle their numb toes

and wrap their icy fingers around steaming mugs.

Sadly it is always the same. They trudge through my "haunted" house and perch themselves near the stairwell where I died. They always leave at dawn, morose, citing proof in bumps and creaks that I never made.

If only they knew.

I have no voice.

Mine is an eternal observation of other's lives. Craving warmth and touch, I enviously watch as snowflakes become flowers, then bees and falling leaves before becoming snowflakes once more.

Mine is an endless winter.

"The Always Engine" Or "About the Winter..." by M.M. Mason

I

Shadow from light: that is how the arrival of the dark form of the ship appeared against the backdrop of the pale winter planet. As disconcerting as it would have been to see, it was the sound that punished: a sonic whip that battered the frozen landscape. Even inside the womb of this towering Earth vessel, Michael always cringed a little. He imagined what the Pellman Drive could do. In the floating harness of his travel frame, he uncomfortably visualised the aural damage as it spread through the alien city, fracturing glass and shuddering the brooding frozen and dead forest and slopping hills that surrounded it. Not today, thought Michael. Not with the most terrible news he had ever broken to a non-terran culture.

The table before him was covered with the traditional consular paperwork, nothing digital. This time the carefully coded and sealed pages were sporadically scattered across the broad slate desk. These were not the usual, even, controlled piles he usually made, inducing small order into the chaos of intergalactic diplomacy. *Must have read it wrong.* Documents were spread like hurricane debris in the trail of churning black clouds. Michael flipped each page with the sharp, irregular movements of denial. He had read it seven times: nothing changed, nothing improved, nothing stopped him from remembering he was the one to explain what had happened to this hapless planet. No diplomat's luxury could pay off this waking nightmare. He pushed a red button to call his colleague in.

"Barbara..." There was no response for a minute. He swallowed. "Barbara..."

"Yeah, Mike, you okay?"

"Please get in here—bring Tosan with you."

"Tosan? Really?" he could hear the smirk in her voice.

"Yeah, 'fraid so. This is one he has to be a part of."

First Security Offer, Barbara Chávez, stepped swiftly in. She gestured away her two security foreman. One asked if she would like Tosan to be collected and sent in. She nodded with a shrug. The first security officer was impressive. She wore a crisp, dark uniform with unbroken charcoal grey lines. The uniform was simple and solid, except for a stunning cluster of medals on her left shoulder that could not be ignored, though many foolishly tried. Dark, peppered hair was closely cropped on her head and a thin scar ran from her forehead and into her hair line. She stopped briefly and looked over Michael's left shoulder.

"Damn...look at that. You alright?" Michael shook his head. They could hear Tosan coming up the hall, complaining to someone about needing to get ready for the native delegation. Tosan was decked out in ceremonial regalia of deep burgundy. A pale yellow sun was centred on his chest. He paused in the doorway. Turning his closely shaven bald head between the two others present he knew something had happened.

"What's up guys? I've got like fifteen minutes and they said I need to be in on this one."

"Tosan, sit down." Michael pointed to a chair across the table. "Shut the door when you come in." Tosan looked nervous now and pressed a button by the door and it hushed shut, veiling the room in an ungentle silence.

Michael, a slender, brown haired man in his mid-forties was silhouetted at the window by a montage of passing alien structures. With a ceremonial steadiness insisted upon by the native culture, the terran transport vessel passed with glacial slowness down the long straight royal promenade. Behind him, a series of tall, dark and narrow structures passed: beautiful and imposing. Each ledge window and corner was covered in pale sheaths of ice and freshly fallen snow. The shadowed silhouettes of hundreds of terrestrial aliens could be seen lining the sacred street as the first Earth visit in twelve years glided down the royal boulevard.

Michael turned back towards them. "What do you two know about the end of the climatic Earth crisis in the previous millennia?

Tosan looked towards Barbara and back to the diplomat. "I'm not really a history guy, Mike. We talked about this." Michael raised his hand to silence him.

Barbara answered cleanly: "We developed some tech that could lower the temperature, but only after millions died." Michael nodded approval of her summation.

"Yes," he added, "after centuries of climatic suffering, we developed a series of Drox-powered machines. Irregular and imperfect as they were, still legal then, they were kept running for nearly a century and...things just kind of turned around." His look was far away. "Worked pretty well, just kept them going, did some maintenance over the decades and things just turned around. They were called Regulators." He shook his head, now looking at the papers on the table. "Kind of innocuous really—that name. Sounds like something you used to keep a primitive vehicle running."

"Mike, what is this about?" Barbara pragmatically pushed him. Tosan looked to them both questioningly. Michael paused for a minute, still thinking.

"When we first came to this planet four centuries ago," he continued, "there was a twelve thousand year old culture. Not as technologically advanced as ours, mind you, no, but a brilliant, complex intellectual culture. Philosophy, art, language...unparalleled really. The wealthy across the empire couldn't get enough of it. Our early traders saw a very desirable commodity: exports of their creative output." He walked over to the window, pointing to the hauntingly beautiful structures that passed.

"Even then we had pretty tight laws about colonising planets like this one, so we didn't. How noble of us. But we could export...by God we could export any and every beautiful thing they offered to our privileged empire. And they offered a lot for what we had." Tosan stirred uncomfortably at this insurgent language. "What we had to trade was technology. Stuff...almost worthless to us by then. Old gear that was centuries obsolete but very, very valuable to this world."

Barbara touched her face, quietly thinking: "Drox technology?"

"Yep," Michael answered.

"There was some Drox *weather* technology in the deal wasn't there?"

"There was," Michael said flatly, his voice trailing off at the end.

Barbara shut her eyes and shook her head.

"What the hell, guys?" Tosan was standing now.

Barbara answered for Michael: "In the unregulated early dump of nearly worthless technology we included some of our early experimental tech for terraforming."

"Yes...and three centuries ago, almost exactly," he looked at them both intensely, "this planet faced a catastrophic drop in temperature that wiped out 87% of Adrarian culture and ended three out of five of this planet's nations. We made a place...colder that didn't need it. It never stopped."

Tosan's eyes were wide. "No...way. That's what that crap says. Seriously?" Michael said nothing now, his back to them, looking out the window. "Wait, you have to tell them that tonight?" Tosan was already edging to the door.

Michael turned back to them: " *We* have to tell them, Tosan."

"Me, why me?" Tosan turned pleadingly to the security officer. She frowned at him. "Of course, you're the Sacred delegate, Tosan. You know good and well that over 20% of native culture has converted, and the other 80% know how religious Earth is and want to get along with us."

Tosan raised his eyebrows, incredulous. He turned back to Michael. "You're the diplomat, Mike. This is your deal. Hey man, I'm not even that religious. You know that. My father said if I took this position it would be ideal for..."

"Shut up!" Michael silenced him.

"I'm going to tell them, damn it, but you have to be there."

Michael turned to First Officer Barbara Chávez. "And you have to keep us alive after I do."

II

The last twenty-five minutes of the journey were spent in heated
planning, three voices rising and falling as diplomatic and
potentially life-preserving tactical decisions were made. When
the steady hum of the transport engine silenced and the vessel
shuddered to an abrupt stop, everyone ceased talking and
turned slowly to the office door.
The forty metre umbilical tube that connected to the Gierioche
Intergalactic Diplomatic Centre had a chemically tainted,
metallic scent that made them cough gently. This atmospheric
mixture was sometimes considered analogous to the semi-salted
brine of an inland oceanic sound, where marine life adapted to
the extremes of fresh water or the salty finality of the deep
ocean. This preparatory tunnel was an atmospheric rite of
passage that finalised human lungs. This was despite seven
months of steady pre-conditioning. Four inches of reinforced
plating separated them from the unforgiving, iron rich
atmosphere of Chuln, and the door was about to open.
Centuries of inter-galactic diplomacy had offered Earth many
harsh lessons, some forgotten and some ignored, but every
government agreed that the cold glare and undeniable
separation of helmet glass was no replacement for a face to face
discussion. Flesh looking on flesh was irreplaceable, even in this
deep and distant basement of the known universe.

III

Michael stood alone in a snow veiled court yard called
the *Serenity Void*. He never knew if it meant there was a void of
serenity or whether it was an empty place where serenity could
be found. With characteristic finality, the alien delegates had
once told him that no perfect translation could be offered in the
human tongue so no more would be tried. This was
pronounced with characteristic Chulnian flawlessness but with

some strange inflection in the comparatively simple language of Earth, what the aliens called *the language of Adam.* Something about this enigmatic and ancient scriptural reference to Genesis always chilled Michael and he could never say why.

With soft white flakes gathering on his shoulders, the diplomat's eyes panned across the unknowable white mounds in the four corners of the wide courtyard. In over two decades of his diplomatic trips to this distant sphere, no one had ever swept away the snow. On one of his five trips, he had decided that this was once a garden and something green and eternal lay beneath the still and patient ice. He imagined verdant, cheerful multi-coloured bushes of a kinder age. *Perhaps not.* Now all that could be seen were the ghostly mounds of an endless winter's downfall.

In the centre, as always, there were the three enigmatic dark buildings. Tall, narrow, elaborately decorated, every inch of their surfaces were immaculately dressed in archaic and beautiful designs. Terrestrial runes told stories of dead heroes and petulant kings and queens that that rose and fell when the world was young. Like most of Chulnian architecture, they remained closed to him and silent like the frozen wastes of this ancient planet. They always insisted on this cerebral, ceremonial wait before a visitor was allowed to enter the senatorial hall where he would speak with the alien delegation and seventeen (always seventeen) representatives of the ancient families. An eighteenth chair always remained empty; something always told him precisely what this emptiness represented, so he never asked.

Michael knew his colleagues, as was customary, would currently be waiting in two separate but identical ice-covered gardens of the botanical dead. What he did not know and had no time to wander was if the centre building in their Serenity Voids was, for the first time, slowly opening.

IV

As dark as the tall narrow centre building was, the open door seemed to glow—the contrast of the light spilling onto the snow seemed as luminous and wavering as light underwater. Late afternoon dressed the image in silence and nothing moved but the thin trail of a distant building's chimney smoke. Some alien's home hearth fire, now a ghost gliding across the late afternoon sky, passed over the distant roofs.

At first Michael stood still. For nearly a minute, stepping closer to the aperture was an impossibility. But then a soft sound emerged: an ephemeral singing that eventually rose through the building and shimmered out across the gently reflective ice. He stepped haltingly forward.

Entering the doorway was disorienting; the inside seemed to stretch forever above him. There was what seemed to be an optical illusion of shrinking lines, like a vertical hallway above. Frame within frame climbed until a light glowed in the heavens of the upper structure and left any living thing beneath it standing in a pool of soft shadow. Around him there was the deep, undying green of a vibrant forest. Plants of varieties unknown to Michael intertwined gracefully up through the tower and he looked for what felt like forever through the emerging shimmer of his swiftly watering eyes.

"Please close the door, Michael." The gentle voice came to him across the bowing flowers and he shook the unexpected emotion shamefully from him, wiping his eyes after what he thought, strangely, was an inexplicably private moment. He shut the door quickly, as the winter waited outside.

"I'm sorry," he started, speaking to the voice. His words carried further than he thought as he searched the narrow forest's heart. Michael raised a hand to gesture apology, but was embarrassed that he could say nothing more.

"Culminitierieth intane lelth..." the words felt to be an offering, a soft gift after the hard edge of terrestrial cold just behind him. Underneath, a sub-note in the alien's throat wavered with the primary pattern of the words. For a moment Michael was speechless, still listening to the music of the speech as it disappeared in the moist light.

"I don't know what that..."

"It means the song of my heart escaped through my eyes." It stood almost next to him: tall, slender, elegant as a deep forest elm, but as pale as the dying of November, and perhaps twice as sad. A unique pattern, like elaborate human freckles, covered the arms in rich and remarkably symmetrical patterns. The upper set of two eyes was set further apart than the two smaller ones just above the slender nose. And the mouth, almost lipless in its monotone, turned up disarmingly at the sides. Some part of him assumed benevolence.

"I don't know how..." he stopped talking for he had not truly stopped crying.

"It is okay. That is what you say isn't it?" The hand touched his shoulder; six long, slender fingers grouped in twos enveloped his upper arm. He nodded, wiping his eyes again.

"Yes, that is what we say." They stood together quietly for a moment looking at the leaves.

"You carry a burden from your world and you wish to lay it at our feet don't you?" He paused briefly in alarm, but eventually he simply nodded slowly.

 "Then tell them."

"You don't understand. It will hurt them. Make them angry..."

"Kirth-polm": the two plosive syllables were abrupt on the lips. This time the sub-note wavered only at the start. Then a straight, strident tone hummed beneath it. The elegant long throat reddened beneath the chin.

"Anger?"

"Yes, that is what it means." It pointed to a wider and narrow screen that could just been seen on the far wall behind a gathering of thin, terrestrial ferns. He saw the alien word, sharp, cruel and spined. Behind it the word *anger* and then a slash and the word *rage*. He had seen these translations plates before: priceless in the early communications between species. Michael

138

looked up now; the eyes of his tall companion looked away. The question escaped his lips before he could stop it.

"You know already?" This time the alien paused, perhaps thinking.

"I do, and only a few more." The tone was now only melancholy.

"How long?" Michael asked pleadingly. The response was quick, crisp.

"Fourteen Earth standard years." For an impossibly long time he could say nothing.

"I am sorry." The creature stood with him, both looking down.

"I know."

"We can fix it..." the alien cut him off.

"You cannot." It was sharp, bitter. "It has been tried and nothing can make a machine touched by *their*...longevity technology." Michael's brow furrowed.

"Their?"

"The ones that were here before us, and you." Michael began to ask but the long slender hand lifted to silence him. The voice was steady, perhaps the recitation of something that had been thought many times before.

"You are not the only ones from whom we took technology. We wanted to never again have to ask you for technology to *help* our world. This was even before we knew you had inadvertently caused it. Such a changed machine will never stop and can never be taken off-world when their technology modifies it."

"I don't know what you—"

"No, you don't." Michael wanted to ask more questions about the *others*, but instead he asked a simpler question.

"What do you call this technology that makes a machine work without stopping?"

"Piastenteln - Ob." There was mysterious and ambiguous note that accompanied the word. Michael turned to look at the translator plate. He saw the translation: always engine.

"Michael there is no more time, so I want you to go to our representatives now and tell them. I have made efforts to make sure you and your team get safely to your ship and safely home, but you will need to get out swiftly as they react. They will...not be pleased." The chilling insufficiency of the words stunned Michael to silence.

"Go now," it said.

"Thank you" he said. Almost forgetting, he asked: "who are you?" It turned back to him before stepping into the leaves.

"I am the *Gardener*" it paused. Considering the word then it spoke in its ancient tongue, now with hauntingly beautiful sub-notes, the word for *Gardener*. "Tialintilth." Then it was gone. Michael quickly turned to the translation plate and said the word Gardener. The alien language translated the word into the wavering elegance of the alien language and offered a second interpretation in italics, the word: "*Queen*".

V

When Michael finished there was a quiet blanket of disbelief on the range of alien faces across the senate floor. He could just barely hear a few distressed and wavering throat noises, in some ways like the notes he had heard from the Queen, but more dismayed and highly pitched. There was also, then, a sound akin to crying in one of the stands which held a range of Chulnian civilians.

Tosan, who had been sitting quietly on his right for the whole speech, now leaned into the microphone. "Yeah, uh Senators, I just want to add that I am really...really sorry too. So...you know." There was an uncomfortable squeak as the microphone fed back. When Tosan noticed Michael and First Security Officer Chávez were staring at him in disbelief, he lifted both his hands: "What?"

A more widespread sound of turmoil and anguish arose from the far corners of the large senate room as the realisation of what they had heard set in. One of the chief senators stood,

140

demanding order from his colleagues. None were listening by this time.

Some parts of the high ceilinged room were veiled in shadow, and from some of the darker recesses of the facility, alien forms emerged speaking fiercely with each other, gesticulating violently at the humans. Michael had never seen this side of them before. Chávez physically urged Michael away from the table, hurrying him towards a rear door. She gestured to someone to Michael's right.

A dark skinned security officer with a determined look began walking towards them. Michael furrowed his brow and stopped. "Wait, Barbara, is that Colonel Phillip Turner?" She looked at the soldier, and nodded.

"Well, yeah..." She tried to physically sweep Michael along. "Turner, the war hero? No way...he's on your detail? Nice one."

"Mike, do you understand what is happening right now? We are not safe here. We have to move and Colonel Turner is going to help make that happen." She looked at Michael with concern, realising he might be somewhat in shock at the situation that was emerging. Colonel Turner approached them rapidly, speaking to some of his subordinates on his head set and gesturing to his subordinates to form a perimeter.

"Madam Chávez, we are most certainly about to face an alien assault. We need to get the Deputy Minister to his transport. I am forming a rear guard now..." She nodded. There was then the sound of what Michael believed to be alien automatic fire somewhere near the senatorial platform and the projectiles disintegrated parts of the right side of the desk where they had just sat. Tosan had both hands on his head and was screaming something. A young priest in a solar robe supported his superior, hurrying Tosan along. One of the soldiers near Michael seemed to be holding his side and dropped down to one knee. Chávez screamed for a medic and drew her side arm. Colonel Turner and two soldiers ran forward towards the surging alien crowd and threw what looked like four or five small plates across the floor towards the senate stand. A wavering blue screen emerged between them. Small arms fire scored across it a moment after as the kinetic energy of terrestrial bullets ricocheted up into the rafters and shredded parts of the patterned floor.

Chávez shouted to Michael above the rising din. "We have been given a message that the monarchy is going to assist our departure..."

"Yeah, I know, the Queen told me." It was her turn to be in disbelief.

"No one has ever seen her. You spoke with the Queen?" He smiled inappropriately.

"Kinda, yeah..." She was now sure he was in shock and began running him towards the rear exit. Then she saw that their escape was being cut off as a mob of furious aliens blocked the exit.

"Heavy ordinance, Madam Chávez," one soldier shouted. "On your six..." Just as they turned to look, a missile shrieked forward, projected from some form of shoulder launcher and the rocket, at too low of an angle, skimmed the ground and bounced with a trail of black smoke just over Michael's right shoulder and impacted deafeningly into the far wall, showering them all in spinning debris. Chávez fired several rounds at the source mere seconds after the botched alien launch.

"Don't kill them..." Michael shouted his voice hoarse. Chávez cursed impatiently as she shoved him towards the opening in the wall, but she did not stop firing. He could see ejected shells pattering across the rich mosaic of the ancient floor.

A moment later they were outside in the night cold. A heavy sleet was falling and flood lights blurred into his eyes.

"Madam Chávez," he heard someone say: "we took the liberty of moving up the mother ship...transport is down." Michael heard more sporadic gunfire and noticed the transport was burning. Behind it, what he thought was the night sky, was the immensity of the earthling mother vessel, awaiting its passengers. Some plasmic discharges arced out from the ship

142

and lit up emerging alien attackers. Only a mist remained where they had stood and their weapons tattered across Chulnian concrete. Human and alien voices ripped through the chaos. "Right, I want them on board now, soldier," Chávez demanded. "You are authorised to use recovery tech. Copy?" There was a brief exchange that Michael tried to understand but further explosions could be heard. He felt a disorienting tug as he was lifted up towards the mother ship. One of the twenty metre rescue arms squeezed the breath out of him and lifted him into the night sky. Sporadic exchanges of fire could be seen in the flashing turmoil fifteen meters below and then he was pulled inside. The security doors hissed closed behind him. He was secure, the silence of the safety room around him. Four dark walls. He sat shaking on the floor. A thought came unbidden as he looked at the ceiling high above him. *There should be flowers.*

VI

The return to Earth left him tired and thoughtful. The things he had seen and heard: they were now the smoke trails and disembodied echoes of his dreams. All of them were the wearied inheritance of his waking moments. But home was home, he told himself, and Michael felt relieved when the ship blasted into existence from their Tran-space journey. There was no damaging sonic whiplash in high orbit—emptiness and now *something,* but no cruel boom of an arriving vessel. Earth citizens would not have it. His jaw tightened with memory. Within minutes the vessel touched down and the extensive crew swiftly unloaded the ship in the warm glow of morning. Instructing a few of his assistants where to take his personal baggage, Michael walked slowly down the platform into the blinding glare of sunrise.

To his left a series of boxes and various elements of scattered cargo were being mounted onto transports. Paying little attention to it, he began walking. One young man in a navy union drew his attention. "Chief Consul, sir..." Michael turned to him absentmindedly.

"Yes..." he looked at the man's arm patch "...Sergeant". The officer pointed to an unusual looking piece of tech that stood near the supply transport.

"Sir, we are having trouble moving this new...component." Michael furrowed his brow.

"I'm not sure why you have come to me for that?" The Sergeant breathed a moment, thinking.

"Well sir, it is not one of ours. I was told it was a gift from the alien delegation." Michael's mouth became very dry.

"Did you say you had trouble moving it?" The sergeant had a confused look.

"Once it touched the ground, we couldn't lift it again...no matter how many of my team pitched in." Michael looked anxiously over the Navy sergeant's shoulder and walked over to the disturbingly smooth and archaically sculpted looking device. There was a simple metal base plate, written in elegant but clear font, meant to be understood by earthling eyes.

"'Piastenteln – Ob', the sergeant read it aloud awkwardly. "Do you know what that means, sir?" Michael's answer was flat, cold, dreadful.

"It means *the Always Engine.*"

The temperature began to swiftly plummet as humanity, like ants climbing on a rotting apple, tried to shut it down. None ever did.

The Christmas Puppy by Mabel Instone

I woke up with a lump on my legs, my stocking full of presents. I leapt out of bed and ran to my sister's room.

"Dee! Wake up! It's Christmas!!"

Her real name was Cordelia and that was what everyone called her. Only I called her Dee.

She woke looking grumpy at first until she realised what I'd said. Then, as they say, her frown turned upside down! We both crept into our parents' room and jumped on their bed,

"PRESENTS!!" we yelled.

Later, Dee and I went out for a walk in the snow. We found a patch of deep, pure untouched snow and ran through it. Dee saw something in the bushes and scrabbled over to find out what it was, disappearing into the snow laden branches. When she didn't come back I went to find her. I pushed through to a sort of clearing in the middle of the bushes to find my sister sitting on the ground holding something. There was snow everywhere else except for a small circle around her. I called to her to try to get her to come back home. It was starting to get dark and we needed to get back. She just sat there examining something in her hands. I knew I should just go and grab her, but I didn't want to go in that circle, something wasn't right. Instead I made a snowball and threw it at her. As the snowball hit her she lifted her head up and was smiling.

"Look at my new friend, Jenny."

She held up the thing she was holding. It was a wooden toy dog with scratches on it. It only had three legs with one was shorter than the others. Its head was tilted and it only had one eye. Then something happened, the bushes shook around us and the snow came falling down on top of us. I crawled out from a pile of snow and pulled Dee up. The toy dog was nowhere to be seen and Dee and I returned home.

That night I fell asleep to thoughts of that wooden dog. The next morning I woke up with a lump on my legs, my stocking full of presents. I leapt out of bed and ran to my sister's room.

"Dee! Wake up! It's Christmas!!"

My sister woke looking grumpy at first until she realised what I'd said. Then, as they say, her frown turned upside down. We both crept into our parents' room and jumped on their bed,

"PRESENTS!!" we yelled.

Hang on... Have I done this before?

We sat on mum and dad's bed and started to open the presents in our stockings. I got a notebook, a new pair of socks, some books and pencils and some sweets, Dee got the same sort of things, but then she opened her last present and it was a wooden toy dog with scratches on. It had three legs with one was shorter than the others. Its head was tilted and it only had one eye. Dee seemed to recognise it too. Suddenly all the memories came flooding back. Had we had Christmas already? I took the toy dog from Dee and hid it in my stocking. Later when dad lit a fire, I threw it in and watched it burn.

Twenty-seven years later I was at my sister's house watching her own kids open their presents. I saw that there was one left under the tree labelled *Dee.* She opened it, confused, she didn't remember it being there before. As she tore off the wrapping paper, something fell out. I picked it up and saw what it was. It was a little wooden toy dog with scratches on it. It had three legs, one was shorter than the others. Its head was tilted and it only had one eye.

RECIPES

Perfect Winter's Supper by Shirley Nelder (Scribbling Scribes Creative Writing Group)

The phone rings.

Hello?

Hi Mum? I am phoning to pick your brains?

Hello Emma. That's nice. Having someone acknowledge that I have a brain is good. Your father always used to say to me 'If you had a brain you'd be dangerous'...

Mum! Concentrate. Matty has just phoned to ask if he can bring a couple of friends home for supper. Of course, I said yes but I've checked the fridge...and it's pretty bare. Any ideas?

Hmm. Well, I well remember you children used to love coming home in the winter to the smell of my *Cheesy Potato Bake.* Do you have any potatoes?

Yes. Plenty of *potatoes.*

What about *bacon, onion and cheese*?

Hold on a minute, I'll check. Yes. Got those.

Right. Here's what you do. *Peel and slice the potatoes thinly, chop up an onion (I prefer red onion but it's not important) and cut the bacon into pieces with a pair of kitchen scissors.* Got it?

Yes, that sounds easy enough. Then what?

Layer the onion, bacon and potatoes and again onion, bacon and potatoes in an oblong dish. Add about 200ml of stock and cover with foil. Bake for an hour at 180C. Remove the foil and check the potatoes are cooked. If they aren't pop it back in for a bit longer. Then grate lots of cheese over the top and put it back into the oven until the cheese has melted. That's it. Simple but really tasty and warming.

Sounds lovely mum. Yes, I can remember those freezing cold wintry days and your delicious potato bake. It'll do very well.

What about putting a milk pudding in at the same time?

As long as it's not of the frog spawn variety. Used to hate that at school. And I can remember dreading finding cook's nails in the apple pies.

Cook's nails? What are you talking about? That is disgusting. I never knew that. I'd have complained if I had.

They weren't actually cook's nails, mum. It's what we called the hard bits of core when we found them. Just like we called sago pudding frog's spawn.

Oh, right. What about a nice creamy rice pudding if you don't like frog's spawn?

Yummy rice pudding - used to have it with a dollop of jam....that is if we had any jam. I know things were tight then. I've got plenty of milk. It can go in with the potato bake. You know what growing lads are like? Never stop eating.

Yes, I remember it all too well. Especially when they have their growth spurts.

Hmm. Anyway, thanks for that mum. I don't suppose you would like to join us? We'll be eating around 5'ish.

That would be lovely, Emma. It gets dark so quickly now. I get a bit lonely here without your dad.

I know mum, it'll be nice to see you. Bye for now...

Bye Emma.

How to make 'Mrs Guinness' Cake' – Polly Beighton

Ingredients

8oz butter
8oz soft brown sugar
10oz plain flour and 2 level tsps of mixed spice sieved together
8oz seedless raisins
8oz sultanas
4oz mixed peel
4oz walnuts (chopped)
8-12 tablespoons Guinness
4 eggs (lightly beaten)

Method

1. Cream butter and sugar together until light and creamy

2. Gradually beat in the eggs

3. Fold in the flour and mixed spice

4. Add the raisins, sultanas, mixed peel, and walnuts.

5. Mix well together.

6. Stir 4 tbsp of Guiness into the mixture and mix to a soft dropping consistency.

7. Turn into a prepared 7inch round cake tin and bake in a very moderate oven (Gas Mark 3/325°F/160°C) for 1 hour.

8. Then reduce heat to a cool oven, (Gas Mark 2, 300°F/150°C. *You may need to cover top of cake when lowering over temperature to prevent it drying out.*)

9. Cook for 1½ hours.

10. Allow to become cold.

11. Remove from tin.

12. Prick the base of the cake with a skewer and spoon over the remaining 4-8 tbsp of Guinness.

13. Keep cake for 1 week before eating.

Friday Night Cheat's Fish Risotto (Serves 2) – Linda Acers

One 350g supermarket fish pie mix

One(or two) fish in butter sauce

1/4 pint of milk (or more if needed)

Half of one 45g packet of cheese sauce powder mix

One (or two packets) of microwave rice – or 120g dry rice cooked

Spinach (optional)

Parmesan cheese

Asparagus or tender stem brocolli (optional)

This is a very quick and easy supper dish and takes 15 minutes max if using dried rice but less if using microwave rice.
Cover the bottom of a saute pan with the milk and poach the fish in it adding the fish in butter sauce.
The fish cooks very quickly.
Mix the cheese sauce mix with a little milk and add to the fish mixture and stir until it thickens slightly. Then add the microwave rice (or cooked boiled rice) and stir in.
Add spinach if using and stir in until lightly cooked.
In the meantime cook the broccoli for around 7 minutes in boiling water or asparagus for 3 minutes in boiling water if you are using either.
Serve the risotto in a pasta bowl with the cooked broccoli or asparagus on top with a sprinkle of parmesan cheese.
(You can use white or wholemeal rice for this recipe and you can also add prawns if you like them.)

Spiced Fruit Cake – Linda Acers

200g margarine
250g dark brown sugar
500g mixed dry fruit
75g candied peel
340ml of water
1 heaped teaspoon of bicarbonate of soda
2 heaped teaspoons of mixed spice
3 large eggs
200g of plain flour
200g of self-raising flour
Pinch of salt

Place margarine, sugar, fruit, candied peel, water, bicarb and mixed spice in a large pan and bring to boil. Simmer for 1 minute. Pour into a large mixing bowl to cool.
Line 2 loaf tins.
When mixture is cool add eggs, flour and salt and mix well and pour into prepared loaf tins.
Bake in the centre of a moderate oven (Gas 4, 350 degrees F or 180 degrees C for about an hour (check after 45 mins to be on the safe side!).
Enjoy!

N.B This recipe has NEVER failed for me and you can swap the fruit ratio around
and use a lighter brown sugar if preferred. I have even used all self-raising flour when I ran out of plain flour and it still works).

OCCASIONAL PIECES

The Winter's Tale by Bruce Hugman

'...a sad tale's best for winter...'
There's a long, tragic winter of suffering in this late play of
Shakespeare's, but it ends in a spring and summer of
reconciliation and optimism; it gives us hope that after dark
days, the sun will shine again. Its themes are jealousy, error,
gullibility, cruelty, the arbitrary exercise of power, the abuse of
women; and, in stark contrast, loyalty, integrity, goodness, the
power of love and the restorative effect of time. It exhibits the
tyranny and foolishness of men and the strength and resilience
of women. Some of its issues are rooted in the period of its
writing – the divine right of kings, absolute regal power and the
obsession with royal heirs (sound familiar?) – but, five hundred
years later, its themes and conflicts are as relevant and
contemporary as ever; it speaks directly to us.
It's a fable, a fairy-story of wicked kings, wrecked relationships,
lost princesses, kind shepherds, honest courtiers and happy
endings, played out through vivid characters, strong emotions
and rich language; a tale that has entertained and enthralled
audiences for centuries.

* * *

Let me tell you the story.

King Leontes of Sicilia suddenly comes to believe – without a
shred of evidence - that his old, dear childhood friend, King
Polixenes of Bohemia, who's been a guest at the palace, has
been having an affair with his Queen, Hermione, and that she is
carrying a child that is not his. He has an extended, profound
paroxysm of jealousy that everyone at court finds inexplicable
and absurd. He throws Hermione in prison and tries to have
Polixenes poisoned.

> *The two kings were like brothers as children.*
> *This is the lovely description Polixenes gives to*
> *Hermione of those days of innocence:*
>   We were, fair
> Queen,
> Two lads that thought there was no more behind
> But such a day tomorrow as today,
> And to be boy eternal ...
> We were as twinned lambs that did frisk i'th'sun,
> And bleat the one at th'other. What we changed
> Was innocence for innocence: we knew not
> The doctrine of ill-doing, nor dreamed
> That any did.
> [I:2, 63]

Leontes' lifelong advisor, Camillo, horrified by being charged
with poisoning Polixenes, spirits the visiting king and his
courtiers out of the country and exiles himself to Bohemia with
them.

Hermione gives birth to a girl. Challenged by his closest
advisors, Leontes sends emissaries to the highest appeal court
on earth – the Sun God Apollo's oracle at Delphi – and
promises to accept the divine verdict on his wife's fidelity and
the parentage of the baby.

Hermione is humiliatingly arraigned at a public trial in which
Leontes throws unsubstantiated capital charges at her. The
verdict of the oracle is delivered: Hermione is innocent and
Leontes entirely in the wrong about everything. With narcissistic
self-righteousness, Leontes declares the oracle false and
condemns Hermione; she collapses and is taken away.
Meanwhile, another loyal courtier, Antigonus, after persuading
the King not to have the newborn princess burnt to death, is
ordered to take the baby and abandon it in some remote,
desolate place, to live or die as Fortune dictates.

News is brought that the child Prince, Mamillius, heir to the throne, previously apple of his father's eye, has died from misery and illness after the disgrace of his mother. She, we are told, soon dies too. Leontes suddenly sees that he is being punished by the gods for his blasphemous rejection of their judgement. He commits himself to a lifetime of repentance. Antigonus, already on the high seas, fulfils his mission, leaving the baby on a distant seashore in Bohemia (where there are actually no seashores, but no matter for that). Following probably the most famous stage-direction in all theatre, 'exit, pursued by a bear', Antigonus is killed and eaten, while his ship and crew are destroyed in a terrible storm.

The baby, along with a bag of gold and documents left by Antigonus, is found by an honest old shepherd, who takes her into his family and brings her up as one of his own.

Sixteen years pass, and the baby princess, Perdita ('the lost one'), has become a beautiful young woman, with no notion of her ancestry. Prince Florizel, son of King Polixenes, engaged in some kind of back-to-nature adventure in the countryside with his falcon, has met her and they have fallen deeply in love. There's a great sheep-shearing festival at which they intend to get engaged. (The jolly, sociable rural party is in stark contrast to the artificiality, formality and peril of the court.)

King Polixenes has got wind of these inappropriate tendencies of his son and heir and, along with Camillo (who'd helped him escape from Leontes), sets out, in disguise, to find out what's going on. They hang around the partying shepherds, but reveal themselves at the point that Florizel and Perdita are about the declare their commitment to each other.

Now it's Polixenes' turn to have a tyrannical fit of regal rage; he brutally rejects his son, threatens to hang him and then to torture, disfigure and kill Perdita for her 'witchcraft'.

Honest and compassionate Camillo steps in once more and manages to evacuate the young lovers and take them secretly back to Sicilia where, he believes, he can convert Leontes and reconcile the wrecked royal families.

And so it comes to pass: when the young couple present themselves at court in Sicilia, Leontes admits his error, accepts Perdita as his daughter and Florizel as his son-in-law; Polixenes retracts his bloody threats when he sees that Florizel is betrothed to a princess. Leontes, after sixteen years of daily penance at his Queen's and son's memorial, is, nevertheless, still wracked with guilt about her death.

Paulina, a lady-in-waiting and wife of Antigonus (who was eaten by the bear), tells Leontes that she has had a wonderful statue of Hermione made in her memory and invites the King to view it. Everyone is amazed at its lifelike qualities but notice that the figure is of a woman much older than Hermione was when she died.

With all the skills of an impresario, Paulina builds up the tension, has music played and invites the statue to come to life and descend from its pedestal. It does; Hermione is alive. King and Queen embrace. In a final flourish of the happy ending, Hermione is reunited with her daughter Perdita and Leontes invites Paulina and Camillo to marry.

* * *

A happy, magical ending, yes, but Mamillius, the heir to the throne, is not brought back to life, nor is Antigonus (Paulina's husband, eaten by the bear) or his entire crew lost at sea. These are the inescapable physical losses caused by weakness and foolishness, never recovered, though they do not colour the play's climax.

In telling the story, even reading the play, aspects of it can seem melodramatic, implausible and over-the-top, but on stage, it's a different matter. The sheer power of the language and the poetry, delivered live, give the characters vivid life and credibility (however exasperating, at times). The full text is tragic, romantic and comic by turns; its events and emotions fairly race forward from the winter of misery to a bright season of the magical and happy ending.

162

* * *

On the way, we see all-powerful, fragile and irascible men indulging their delusions at the expense of the lives and happiness of others; fathers capable of rejecting their children and visiting horrors on them; established, faithful relationships discarded on a whim. On the other hand, honest, compassionate men and women at court plead for good sense and do their best for others, even at great risk to themselves. Open, sociable, rural society is contrasted with the tense, status-conscious relationships of the court; the fragile mental state of those in power is set against the firm, deep maturity and good sense of decent people without pretensions, both at court and in the countryside.

> *Brave Paulina speaks her mind to Leontes,*
> *fearless of his royal anger:*
>
>   O thou tyrant,
> Do not repent these things, for they are heavier
> Than all thy woes can stir. Therefore betake thee
> To nothing but despair. A thousand knees,
> Ten thousand years together, naked, fasting,
> Upon a barren mountain, and still winter
> In storm perpetual, could not move the gods
> To look that way thou wert.
> [III:2,215]

Camillo, trusted advisor to Leontes, then to Polixenes, twice defies his royal masters when he sees that they have gone seriously astray and that disaster looms; he sees the path of justice and goodness and takes it, hazardous to his life though it might be. Paulina, Hermione's companion, is a tower of eloquent, womanly strength. Regardless of the extreme peril of criticizing her King, she calls him out over his insane jealousy, both when Hermione is still alive, and at the very end when she is about to be restored. It's powerful stuff and a vivid display of indignation at the foolishness of men and the oppression of women.

* * *

The Winter's Tale is not the 'sad tale' that the child Prince Mamillius volunteers to tell his mother (a tale of 'sprites and goblins') – Leontes cuts that short by storming on stage and brutally accusing Hermione of adultery. But it is a sad tale of weakness, insecurity, obstinacy and the arbitrary exercise of royal power, particularly men's power over the fate of women. The storm that destroys Antigonus' ship and crew, and the bear that eats him, are instances of the implacability of nature, for which there is no remedy. Implacability in human affairs is shown to be unnatural and dangerous; Leontes claims to be victim of an 'infection', but it is his weakness and his choice, no external agent, that are his downfall.

> *When Leontes is ordering Camillo to burn the*
> *newborn princess, we see into the darkest reaches*
> *of his flawed character:*
> Away with it! ...
> And see it instantly consumed with fire...
> If thou refuse...
> The bastard brains with these my proper hands
> Shall I dash out. Go, take it to the fire.
> [II:3, 131]

The rural community in which Perdita is brought up by the old shepherd, who found and adopted her, represents a colourful and entertaining vision of a bucolic world; open-heartedness and spontaneity flourish close to nature, but there is also complexity and diversity in the characters and their relationships. There is Autolycus, an opportunistic peddlar, thief and pickpocket who scams and exploits his poor, credulous neighbours with engaging aplomb, entertaining them while he cuts their purses. Among the worthless baubles and bric à brac he sells, he carries newly written ballads about supposedly amazing, recent events that he swears are true and which the country folk clamour to hear – the memes of Elizabethan networks.

There is the clown, the old shepherd's son (whom modern jargon might class as neuro-diverse) who struggles to make sense of life's complexities, is easily gulled, and endearingly thrilled when good things happen to him.

* * *

The sheep-shearing festival is an amusing, joyful, communal affair, but it is the love of Perdita and Prince Florizel that crowns the scene with the intensity of its poetic, pastoral romance.

Though the young lovers' happiness is sealed in the end, the play reminds us that even the most intense of relationships can be broken: the childhood friendship of Leontes and Polixenes, is described as the perfect union of young souls: yet even this can be shattered by the weakness and foolishness of adulthood. What has clearly been a passionate and beautiful, life-long marriage between Leontes and Hermione could fall apart instantly at the first hint of jealousy. A father's life-long love for his son could be negated by a single act of filial defiance and lead to threats of the most dreadful punishments. Apparently stable, sane individuals can collapse into monsters in a minute.

* * *

Next to these unstable characters are individuals of unimpeachable honesty, integrity, loyalty and courage, especially Paulina and Camillo, and Hermione herself, all of whom are willing to take any risk, even that of death, for what they know is right and true.

Hermione's defence during the public, mock trial is as eloquent a plea as one can imagine; beautifully written, it touches the heart. Here is just a glimpse:

You, my lord, best know –
Who least will seem to do so – my past life
Has been as continent , as chaste, as true,
As I am now unhappy; which is
More than history can pattern, though devised
And played to take spectators. For behold me,
A fellow of the royal bed, which owe
A moiety of the throne, a great king's daughter,
The mother of a hopeful prince, here standing
To prate and talk for life and honour 'fore
Who please to come and hear...
[III:2, 31]

While Leontes endures his sixteen-year winter of misery and regret in the sterility of his palace, Perdita is flourishing under the benign parentage of the old shepherd in the rich and productive embrace of nature and rural life. In the end, it is the passage of time, and goodness and simplicity that bring about reconciliation and restore integrity and harmony.

The Winter's Tale and the modern world

The destruction of what is beautiful and the disruption of the natural order are themes that are painfully relevant to us. In the dark winter of our current crises, *The Winter's Tale* gives us glimpses of the human follies that take us to perilous places, but also gives us hope that there are ways to find redemption.

We see that the unchecked, irrational, selfish obsessions and pursuits of the powerful wreak havoc with relationships and with society; that the powerful are prone to wild and arbitrary judgements and decisions that destroy their own security and peace of mind as well as the lives of others.

There are examples of such tyrants and fools in every part of the world, some of them leading great nations. They may not kill their own wives or children, but they oversee the disruption of justice, the oppression of multitudes and the death of millions. Tyrants and fools believe whatever suits them, whatever evidence to the contrary there may be.

We see fathers, in whose righteousness and sense of entitlement lie the seeds of violence and cruelty; fathers who threaten to torture and burn their offspring for no offence of their own (the baby princess) or for an assertion of individuality (Florizel). And one of those fathers, Leontes, plans the most terrible death for his own wife, the mother of his heir.

We do not have to look far to similar wickedness in 2021: women stoned for adultery; baby girls exposed on mountains to die; gay sons or daughters expelled from families or whipped or killed by mobs or the state; whole communities persecuted or exterminated for their difference: this merely an abbreviated list of the atrocities perpetrated by patriarchal societies and unhinged men and their obsessions.

In contrast, there are people whose character and behaviour are admirable, models from whom there is much to learn. Camillo, the courtier who speaks his mind, face-to-face with the King, asserting the error and injustice of his beliefs and actions and exiles himself rather than compromise. Paulina, the feisty, powerful companion of the Queen, who eloquently exposes the powerlessness of women against the tyranny of men and invites death as preferable to keeping silent. And in that other world of rural simplicity, Prince Florizel, who will do nothing but follow his love, at any cost, at the expense of everything else, status, riches, royal approval, a kingdom. These are people of character, integrity and courage who will stand firm against the direst odds.

> *Prince Florizel's passion for Perdita is wonderfully*
> *expressed through this hymn to her perfection:*
> What you do
> Still betters what is done. When you speak, sweet,
> I'd have you do it ever; when you sing,
> I'd have you buy and sell so, so give alms,
> Pray so, and, for the ord'ring your affairs
> To sing them too; when you do dance, I wish you
> A wave o'th'sea, that you might ever do
> Nothing but that—move still, still so,
> And own no other function. Each your doing,
> So singular in each particular,
> Crowns what you are doing in the present deeds,
> That all your acts are queens.
> [IV:4. 135]

In terms of what we know of our world, the uplifting end of the play may seem a mere fantasy: a tyrant recognizing the error of his ways and doing penance through sixteen years of regret and misery; an abused and vilified queen, assumed to be dead, restored to her reformed husband; a rejected and long-abandoned child returned to her parents; the reconciliation of old friends, after the poisoning of their relationship, through the betrothal of their children; recognition and respect for the courtiers - the whistleblowers of their time - who held firm. But in our dark times, the passing of the wintry story of the play, the coming of the bright sunshine of the rural interlude and the summer of the ending may lift our hearts and give us hope: that

168

the powerful may come to their senses; that formality and
pretension may not resist the energy of goodness and nature;
that just and generous human relations really do lie at the base
of everything we might dream of.

*

A Mythic Christmas by Ayd Instone

For me the magic always started with All Hallows Eve, the night before All Saints Day, The 1st November which marks the first day of the New Year for the Kalends (who gave us the name Calendar), the Celtic peoples, and the way of the Wicca. It is from the Celts that we have the concept of 'eve 'as they considered the evening, as in from dusk before the important day, to be as revered as much (if not more) than the day itself. On this eve the veil between the worlds becomes so thin, that souls can pass between from that world to this. It was said that on Hallowe'en, witches, or those with the sight, could make use of the superimposing of the worlds to see things that are yet to be. If a young girl lit a candle at midnight and looked into the mirror, over her shoulder she will see an image of her future husband. Visit the graveyard at midnight and you will see the ghosts of those that will die in the coming year. I'd stayed up late on that night many a year. I'd been bold enough to visit a cemetery on some occasions but not a single soul traversed the graveyard while I was there and I saw no future spouse in the mirror. One Hallowe'en though, did I see a coven of around seven witches flying high overhead, silhouetted against the sky at sunset? Perhaps I did.

I'd spent my childhood believing and searching for the magic which seemed to be just around the corner towards the end of each year as we approach Christmas. But in modern times, as the long hoped for snow never appears to replace the drabness of the rain, and as life gets busier and busier, we may be forgiven for thinking the magic is gone, if indeed it was ever there.

Christmas 'critics make the mistake of worrying that the over commercialisation has diluted the spiritual significance or that the religious aspect is irrelevant to them and doesn't apply. A woman in America, after seeing that a local church was advertising a Christmas service was reported to have said "Even the Church is cashing in on it these days." Yet it seems that paradoxes such as these are what give Christmas its fascinating nature. Even in the cynical wonder-less world of twenty-first century there is still magic to be had – if you know where to look. I believe I have found it in the origins and myths that show that Christmas (as we may as well call it) is older than Charles Dickens, older than Jesus, as old as we are, and as old as time itself. Essentially it is this concept of time that it has always represented for humanity, in many different guises, now amalgamated into its current form, with a same essential purpose: to mark the passage of the year, a celebration of survival and a hope for a future. It is these desires that forged the myths that when put together make Christmas.

There are three ways to look at the stories of the past. The most obvious is history: events that happened exactly as described. Then there are legends. A legend is a story that has its roots in history but has become famous through embellishment, not everything about the story may be true or historical. Then there are myths. Mythic events are definitely not historical but are completely truthful, even if they are not literally true. By this we mean that myths explain who we are and where we come from in a way that is totally real and useful but not in any way historical. I propose that Christmas is almost pure myth, with a few legends thrown in, and a sprinkling of history. And therein lies the magic.

Our story starts and ends with light. Before we even get to December there is, in the Hindu, Sikh and Jain world, the festival of lights. It is the story of the fall of a demon named Narkasura, who managed to acquire such awesome powers that he began to terrorise the three worlds until his defeat and death at the hands of Krishna, an avatar of Vishnu. This is celebrated as Diwali. The word Diwali is a shortened version of Deepavali, which means 'cluster of lights'. There is a universal need in all cultures throughout history, following the season of harvest to preserve light at this every increasingly dark time of the year and ensure the return of the sun. In Ireland there is the visit to the Cave of the Sun, An Liamh Greine, now called New Grange, built 5000 years ago, 500 years before the pyramids of Giza and 1000 years before Stonehenge. Stonehenge itself, built around 3100 BCE, is aligned in the direction of the sunrise of the summer solstice and the sunset of the winter solstice.

In these enlightened secular commercial modern times, with electric light illuminating the darkness and central heating removing the chill at the flick of a switch, we may well wonder if there really is any need for a winter festival at all. Is there nothing to the magic of Christmas other than our culturally agreed nostalgia? Nothing but an agreed date in the diary?

Why does Christmas fall on the 25th of December anyway, four days after the winter solstice? Was that really the date of the birth of Christ? The first Gospel to be written, Mark, written AD 66 to 74, doesn't even mention Jesus' birth. The other two synoptic Gospels, Matthew (written AD 70 to 110) and Luke (written around AD 85) can't agree on the details. The last Gospel to be written, John (written AD 90 to 100), ignores it completely. This is unsurprising as the Jews held the date of your birth with little regard, birthdays were not celebrated even if they could be remembered (for ordinary people they were not). The early Christians though were keen to point out the fulfilment of Hebrew prophesy in Jesus in his role as the Jewish Messiah which needed his linage to the legendary King David. It also became important to fix Jesus in a time and a place. If He was God made flesh he would have to have been born and that birth would have had to have been foretold. This ruled out the alternative theories, gaining in popularity at the time, that Jesus was just a man who became the Christ at his baptism or that he arrived on Earth fully grown and fully God in human form as a sort of spiritual avatar. So the Christmas story became an integral part of doctrine to refute these two theologies, becoming almost as important as the Easter story.

173

In AD 336 following the first Council of Nicaea, the 25th of December was fixed as the birth of Jesus by the first Christian Roman Emperor, Constantine. That date had been celebrated by Christians for over one hundred years by then, Constantine just made it official. It became a national celebration in Britain in AD 567 when the Council of Tours declared the twelve days as festaltide. King Ethelred ordained it to be a time of peace when all strife must cease in AD 991.

But why this date in the first place? Is it a Christianisation of a previous festival? The Roman festival of the god Saturn, Saturnia, ran from 17th December to the 23rd, overlapping with the festival of Sol Invictus, which had originated in Syria. An official celebration of Sol Invictus was then officially set to the 25th December in AD 274, long after the date was already being used by Christians. Was it then the opposite, a Romanisation of an earlier Christian festival date?

Jesus was long thought to have been conceived and crucified on the same date, the Vernal Equinox, on 25th March, when the angel Gabriel appeared to Mary and she conceived by the Holy Spirt. Nine months later is the 25th December, so that became Jesus' birthday.

As Rome became Christian, the god Saturn was not completely abandoned. He became a fallen god, a laser being who now bowed to the greater authority of Jesus and swore to no longer demand the rumoured child sacrifice of pre-Roman times. (It is unlikely child sacrifice actually happened. There were Gladiatorial events which resembled sacrifices and pigs offered in temple ceremonies. Later Christians viewed both of these activities as distasteful and exaggerated them.) In his new fallen role and new allegiance, Saturn even turned up at the nativity as one of the wise men from the East, bearing gifts for the infant Saviour.

The giving of gifts can be found in both Saturnia and in the older Kalends festival. The wise men or Magi of the Chaldeans (they were not like to be kings) were likely astrologers and magicians and were twelve in number, not three, but they did

174

bring three gifts: gold for a king, myrrh for a healer (also used as an embalming ointment for the dead), and frankincense for a priest - three gifts representing the three roles of the Christ.

Saturnia was a week-long festival of gluttony, fun, naughtiness, revery, drunkenness and gambling games. Every part of it was adopted into Christmas as the the pagan festival and the Christian one united under the new name. One interesting remnant of Saturnia survives in The Feast of Fools or the Lords of Misrule where the lowest among the citizens become king. The roles are reversed at Christmas, as they were in pagan Rome. Children become bishops and slave owners become slaves. Little Jack Horner who sat in the corner, pulled out a plum representing the choice of king (or perhaps sacrifice) by lot. The same is done by putting a coin in the pudding, a way to randomly select the king of fools.

The Hunting of the Wren is a modern echo of the myth of child sacrifice of hideous earlier times, also encoded in the myth of the massacre of the innocents when Herod ordered the murder of all children in Bethlehem under the age of two to rid himself of the chance of a baby being born as King of the Jews to replace him. Jesus and his family escaped into Egypt. Today we often forget the festival of Childremas, or Holy Innocents Day, on the 28th of December. This event itself is a re-working of the Pharaoh of Egypt's mythical attempt to kill the children of Israel in which Moses escapes, as told in the book of Exodus.

The great god Saturn, lord of agriculture, went by another name of The Holly King, the God of the Waning Year or the Dark Lord. He pulls his hood back to reveal his one good eye and one missing eye. The missing eye sees unmanifest realities. Often wearing a mask, his disguises include the serpent, the eagle, the raven, the wolf or the bear. The Holly King is the Lord of the Winterwood and dark twin of the waning year. He rules from Midsummer to Midwinter, representing withdrawal, life lessons and rest, sometimes with the nickname of Grandfather Frost. He is often accompanied by ravens. The raven being the most cunning of birds, known to folk the world over as a creator and

175

trickster spirit. A raven is inconspicuous in his blue-black mantle, and one can expect to find ravens almost anywhere but most notoriously they were found haunting gallows or as battlefield scavengers, blackening the fields where the slain lay, croaking ominously.

The Holly King's nemesis is his twin, the golden Oak King, the God of the Waxing Year and the Divine Child and Lord of the Greenwood. He rules from Midwinter to Midsummer. The Oak King represents growth and expansion. He is akin to gods such as Jupiter, the Roman god of light and sky, Janus, the Roman god of planting, marriage, birth and other types of beginnings. Red, green, yellow and purple are his colours. His oak is swathed in mistletoe and perching in its branches is the robin. At Midwinter, the Oak King goes to battle with his twin the Holly King for the favour of the Goddess. He slays the Holly King, who does not fully die but goes to rest in Caer Arianrhod until they do battle once again at Midsummer.

There are similarities here to Wodan or Odin, also called Wodan, Woden, or Wotan, one of the principal gods in Norse mythology and who was the great magician among them, associated with runes and poets. In outward appearance he was a tall old man with flowing beard and only one eye (the other he gave in exchange for wisdom by looking into the well of knowledge). In this fitting guise the Elder God is a familiar figure in many folk tales: the wandering Wizard leaning on a graven staff. His purpose is to preserve order and balance in the world. He is God of the Wild Hunt, or Furious Host and is seen to lead spectral horsemen. From ancient times he has been seen leading a tumultuous throng of these skeletal huntsmen, horses and hounds through the autumn night sky, riding himself an eight-legged spider-horse.

The Holly and the Oak King merged with Saturn, Wodan and the Turkish Saint Nikolaus to become the mythic Father Christmas. Saint Nicolas is a reverend grey-haired figure with flowing beard in bishop's raiment and gold embroidered cape, mitre and pastoral staff. In his mortal life he was the Bishop

176

of Myra in the first half of the 4th century and participated in the important first Council of Nicaea in AD 325, ordered by Constantine, which decided the orthodoxy of Early Christianity and the formation of the canon of the New Testament. These decisions cast out the mystery religions and the esoteric Gnostics along with their texts, into the wilderness of oblivion until our re-discovery of them in the Nag Hammadi scrolls in 1945.

After saving numerous poor girls from a life of prostitution by dropping money down their chimneys into their stockings, Saint Nickolas, whose feast day is celebrated on the 6th December, was rewarded with immortality to repeat his gift-giving every year, sat astride a white reindeer. Sometimes he is seen conversing with an angel, the Christkindl, the strange spirit of Jesus yet unborn. The good saint's outfit has changed over the centuries, from gold in the east to green in the west as he merged with the Green Man and Pan, the shaman or spirt of the woods and of the evergreen with a crown of laurel and holly on his head. In northern Europe he wore a hood, surrounded by fur. The hood is a magical artefact, remembered in the game of Blind Man's Buff or Hood Man Blind, the art of disguise and magical knowledge and inner sight. In the New World of the Americas the hood became a bobble cap and the green suit became red and perhaps some of the mystery and magic was lost as he became first a jolly old elf, then just a fat man by the name of Santa Claus.

In Europe, Father Christmas does not work alone. The straw clad ghosts of the field go before the saint clearing the way with whips and flails. Perchta and Berchta are two spirits helpers. Wearing hideous masks, they follow Saint Nicholas distributing nuts and fruit to the good, and screeches to the bad. They carry the saint's big book in which are noted all the things, both good and bad, that the children have been up to during the year, knocking on doors to enquire about the behaviour of the children. They then examine and test the children who have to deliver a song, or otherwise show their skills. There is also Klaubauf, a shaggy monster with horns, who follows Saint

Nikolaus. He carries the presents for the good children. But beware Bartel the Krampus. He is a frightening being with fiery eyes and a long red tongue. He is covered in bells and dragging chains, carrying a bucket containing birch sticks and lumps of coal for naughty children, scaring and punishing those who have not been nice. In some Scandinavian regions, the dark and sinister antithesis of Father Christmas has the name of Ruprecht who comes out of the ancient world, a figure clad in a tattered robe with a whip and a big sack on his back in which he will take children to be sacrificed. Then there is the Mari Llwyd, a hideous horse skull and mummers artefact, brought to the door of children to ask them riddles. The Mari Lwyd, or the grey mare, represents the donkey turned out of its stall to make way for the birth of Christ. Believed to bring good luck and fertility to the houses they visit and those who are touched by them even if the sight of this prowling monster peeping around into the room or pushing it through an upstairs window was the stuff of nightmares. Be careful if you stay up late on the night of the 24th, with this Father Christmas and all his minions loose, you may just catch a glimpse of an anthropomorphism of one of the few ancient primal forces still left in the world.

The Winter Solstice was also considered the birthday of Mithras, the secret ancient Persian god of goodness and light, about whom little is known. Again originating around Syria and Iran, like the Sol Invictus festival, he become a patron god of the Roman occupation troops in Judea before and just after the birth of Christ.

To pagans of most backgrounds and traditions, the Sun represents the male God, and its death and rebirth on the Winter Solstice is seen as the death of the old solar year and the birth of the new, or the birth of the Divine Child, the Sun God of the new solar year. It was an easy switch for the unconquered sun of Sol to become the unconquered son in the figure of Jesus.

To the Egyptians, the sun god was Horus, Divine Child of Isis and Osiris. The world's first attempt at monotheism began with the Pharaoh Akhenaten (Tutankhamun's father) who

178

changed his name from Amenhotep IV to Akhenaten, meaning Effective Spirit or Service of the Aten. The Aten is the solar disc of the sun. He build a new capital at Thebes, banned all other gods and began a worship of the one god in the form of the sun. The Egyptian hierarchy hated him and forced him and his followers to flee into the desert. After his death, almost all memory and artefacts baring his heretical name were destroyed and polytheism returned to Egypt. Some scholars point out the similarities between the historical Akhenaten and the mythological Moses, one of the key founders of Judaism who after hearing Yahweh speak to him from a burning bush, led a revolt in Egypt and took his followers into the desert. Their parallel stories take place at the same time in history, but there is only archaeological evidence for one of them.

To the Greeks and Romans the son god was also Apollo, son of Zeus and twin brother to Artemis, the goddess of the Moon; to Norse and to the Anglo-Saxons he was Balder; to the Phoenicians, Baal; and to the Celts, Bel. In Celtic lore, the Sun-God rules the seasons. At Yule, he is the new babe, the embodiment of innocence and joy. He represents the infancy of the returning light. The word Yule means wheel, the wheel of the year returning to its starting point. At Samhain, he waits in the Shining Land to be reborn in heathen rites (heathen from 'heath-dweller', or country folk).

But enough of all these male gods. What of the goddess? Goddess worship predates male gods by many millennia. Upper Palaeolithic figurines, cave paintings, and other archaeological finds have been found all over Europe, the Middle East and Africa dated as far back as 30,000 BCE.

The twin golds of the Holly and Oak king that each rule for half of a year, fight for the favour of the Goddess. The defeated twin is not truly dead, he merely withdraws for six months to Castle Arianrhod, the Castle of the ever-turning Silver Wheel of the Stars in the Aurora Borealis. This is the enchanted realm of the Goddess Arian where the god must wait and learn before being born again. She is the goddess of the astral skies, the Lady Arian, and there she rules as goddess of reincarnation. The Romans called her the Cailleach - old woman of winter. They equated the Cailleach with their goddesses Juno. The last sheaf of the harvest season was dressed with a ribbon and hung up on a nail until Spring as 'the Veiled One' in honour of the Cailleach. Many tales have her turning into a beautiful young woman in the spring, to wander in her secret woods where in lies her miraculous Well of Youth. In this aspect, she often appears as the faery lover who initiates the individual into the mysteries of the Otherworld. There is the Scottish ballad of Thomas the Rhymer, the story of Thomas of Earlston who was playing music beneath a hawthorn tree on a faery hill. The hawthorn is often found at the borderland between the worlds and is especially sacred to the faeries. Thomas' tunes attracted the beautiful Queen of Elfland who rode up on her white horse. He joined her to ride through a beautiful orchard, but the Queen warned him that if he ate any of the fruit, his soul will burn in the fire of Hell. This was the Tree of Life that stands at the centre of the Celtic Otherworld, and to eat of its fruit means never to return to the mortal world again. They rode on to where the road branched into three. The Queen explained that the narrow path, beset with thorns and briars, is the path of righteousness, and leads to heaven. The broad, smooth road leads to Hell. The third bonny road will take them to fair Elfland, their otherworld destination. She gave him a suit of green elven clothes and bestowed upon him the gift of prophecy and a tongue that could never lie. He had no choice but to trust the Queen and she did indeed protect him, warning him away from acts that would keep him imprisoned in Elfland for ever and saving him from being taken by the Devil.

Every mythology features a Tree of Life, perhaps based on the earlier knowledge of dryads, or tree spirits. In the biblical account of the Hebrew Torah and the Old Testament, based on the older Sumarian epic of the Enuma Elish, the jealous deities of the Elohim, (usually translated the singular Lord God, although plural terms remain in some passages), are greatly angered when the humans eat of the fruit of the tree of knowledge of good and evil, of self-awareness and of consciousness. The gods then set a flaming sword which turned every way, to block the way of the Tree of Life. The race of Adam, of Man, then had to leave Eden to find another way back to the garden and to a life of joy, now with the burden of consciousness, free will, pain, death and sin on their mortal flesh.

The tradition of adorning a tree to represent the tree of life with multi-coloured globes representing the many varieties of worlds pendent from the branches is ubiquitous, although the meaning has long been lost. There is Evergreen Day remembering Adam's act of bringing a scion from the tree of knowledge and planting it giving rise to the species of evergreen trees. One of these became the tree that Christ's cross was made from. The evergreen represents resurrection, where life never dies.

A hymn is usually sung to the tree, wishing it good health and long life in the ritual of wassailing . A blessing is also bestowed upon it to be fruitful; then some loud noise is made in order to drive off any woeful spirits. Toasts to the tree are then drunk from the wassail bowl. When all have finished their toasts, the remainder of the liquid is poured out on the earth around the trunk while bread or cakes from the wassail celebrations are placed upon its branches as decorations.

Christmas is as you can see, is as inter-wovenly multi-cultural as you can get. Just think of elements from the modern traditional Christmas day: the turkey; an Aztec bird, a German tree, a pudding made from Asian spices, a carol about the Bohemian King Wenceslas to the tune of a Swedish spring song, pagan magic, mistletoe and holly, wood spirits dressed up as angels and a Turkish saint. Christmas has had many traditions over the millennia and has proved notably stubborn to give any of them up.

Christmas has a power, stronger than Cromwell who had it banned, only for it to survive underground and resurface when the coast was clear. It is from those sixteen years when public celebration was outlawed in Britain that the concept of spending Christmas with the family became a new tradition, which continues today.

During the agricultural age the twelve days of Christmas, from Christmas Day on the 25th of December to the Epiphany on 6th January (the Eastern Church's calendar put the Vernal Equinox on the 6th April for Christ's conception and therefore his birth on 6th January) were granted as a holiday, but in the industrial age of recent centuries, the holiday shrunk, and continues to shrink to the bare minimum. The erosion of Sunday as a day of rest in recent years and twenty-four hour shopping has reduced the communal rest to levels unheard of since the Victorian workhouses.

Christmas is criticised for sentimentality and yet it is that sentiment that becomes good-will and charity at a time when those in need have greater need than any other time of the year. This Christmas sentiment is most notable in the phenomenal story of Christmas 1914 when the slaughter stopped in the trenches of the Great War and enemies exchanged cigarettes and food and played a game of football. Christmas sentiment was the trigger, initially on the German side, to question the war. The truce lasted several days and in some areas for number of weeks. Only when the generals ordered fraternising with the enemy to be punishable with death did trust turn to suspicion and the guns started booming again. (Alfred Anderson, who served with the 5th Battalion the Black Watch, was the last surviving member of the Christmas Truce. He died in November 2007 aged 109.)

Christmas was and is the perfect marriage of our needs and desires, both ancient and modern. It is the ultimate festival, providing the greatest sense of occasion of all. It is an agreed, shared, communal lift. It is today as it was in ancient times: the festival of birth, of hope, of light, in the black barren darkness of winter. In our electric lit, atmospherically controlled world we have no obvious physical needs, but are there other needs? Does the festive season lighten the darkness in our hearts? Perhaps it does remind us of a Golden Age, whether it is the mythical Victorian Christmas, a primordial Eden, the desire for the certainty of the bicameral mind and the voices of the gods, or perhaps our own childhoods if they were more tranquil than our current lives. It is a celebration of the family and of friendship. A time of greed and yet of charity. A time, as in the trenches of 1914, of questioning the world. It is a deadline, a marker, representing the achievements of the past year and all the hopes and dreams of the years to come, like standing on the edge of eternity. Overall it is special, relieving us from the ordinariness of the rest of the year, so that for a very short time the leaden weight that oppresses us is somehow lifted to reveal our natural state of joy.

Once, when I was a boy, long ago, on around my forth or fifth Christmas Eve, did I see a heavenly faerie host, dressed in gold, flying overhead, singing 'rejoice, rejoice, rejoice!'? Perhaps I did.

Also by T. L. Williams